First Time
Ooh-la-la!

Barry Able

New Generation Publishing

Chapter One

The College Chapel clock was chiming a quarter to ten as Big Jo finished applying her lipgloss and began arranging table and chairs for the term's second meeting of *The Virgins*. This session had to go well. No one had been re-elected President for longer than two terms, and she had set her heart on being there for three. She had, after all, the perfect room for these occasions, the biggest in the whole college, daddy's monthly allowance permitted her to provide bubbly of the highest quality, and her tally of men was impressive even by *Virgin* standards. Tonight looked like a dream: two admissions, one of them indebted to her for the rise to College fame, a well-prepared late session with the *Monks, and* she had managed to acquire a rather special gown for the evening. Yes, a real dream.

On the other side of the quad the Dean was staring in dismay at the coat-hanger on which his legendary ancient gown usually hung. 'How can I possibly break up the session without being properly attired?' he demanded of the Bursar. The latter, who was focussing his field glasses on Big Jo's window, ignored him.

The Dean was already feeling semi-undressed.

'It must have been that Smithson,' he whined, 'he's the last man I had in here. Wretch. He'll pay for it.'

'Calm down,' replied the Bursar, 'just have a look at this. That girl is exceptionally well endowed. That's what we used to call a "perky pair" in the City, you know.'

The Dean grabbed his own glasses. '"Perky pair", eh? Hmmmm…' He sometimes doubted the Bursar's tales of life in the City, and regularly speculated on why such an apparently brilliant financial wizard had decided to leave it. But on this occasion he had to agree. 'Yes. That does sum her up very nicely. Now, how much longer before they start?'

'Ten minutes. I can see one of them in the quad now.

Brazen hussy. Look at the length of that skirt! That's what we used to call…'

'Yes, yes,' said the Dean, refocussing his glasses. 'Let's just call her a brazen hussy. Good god! Never mind, we'll get them when they're sozzled. The amount of alcohol consumed in this College is a disgrace.'

'Hmm,' purred the Bursar. 'But the Bar accounts are in profit for a change, so the Fellows' port is still secure. I've managed to channel a little bit more towards free pre-prandial sherry, by the way.'

'You're the best Bursar we've had for years,' acknowledged the Dean. The Bursar smiled as he took another large swig of the claret. He dragged his hand across his mouth to get rid of the drips and let out a modest belch.

Big Jo scattered a few more of the shimmering stars for which she was famous over her bare shoulders and between her perky pair, and then began lighting the candles.

'Damn,' said the Dean. 'She's probably going to switch off the light. Wretch. That'll spoil my photos.'

But Jo was preparing for the best meeting of *The Virgins* in their five-year history, and by the time her twelfth candle was lit, the view from opposite was teasingly bright. There were two elections tonight, to replace two final years who had decided it was time to 'go steady'. Huh! They'd be stuck with a mortgage and two kids before long. Jo had quite a way to go before that! As she smugly lit the thirteenth candle, there was a knock on the door and Blondilocks, Vice-President, swirled in, tossing her trade-mark hair provocatively and scattering her heavy scent. No style, thought Jo to herself contentedly. Blondi was fine as V-P, but would never make the top job.

'Got the agendas?' asked Jo.

'Sure,' drawled Blondi. 'Shall I open the first bottle?'

'No,' countered Jo. 'We'll pull out three corks together

2

and let the college know who really knows how to do it.'

Blondilocks smiled approvingly and enviously, making a mental note for when she took over. She had a bit of bombshell tonight, after all, no need to spoil the party yet. But she'd just had to finish off writing an essay, and she was rather thirsty. And she could never resist the sort of champagne that Big Jo provided...

The Chapel clockwork whirred into action again and before the tenth hour had struck, all eight *Virgins* were in the room. Apart from Jo, all in their undergraduate gowns, and most in very little besides... This was a society that knew how to run itself! Jo suppressed her delight. Her third term was looking even firmer. 'Let's have these corks all out in the same second,' she ordered, motioning Blondi, Susie and Rocky towards the bottles. She herself took a step towards the window, thought better of it, and instead commanded Emma to open it wide. 'Ready?' she asked the openers. 'I want to wake up those repulsive swots in the library. That place is getting to be the second busiest place in Oxford on a Saturday night – alongside Jesus bar.' Her prepared wit drew appreciative titters, which turned into a cooing of satisfaction as all three corks somehow got their timing right and two of them managed to fly out of the window into the night.

'Rich little brats!' gasped the Bursar as he reached for the decanter of Tuesday night's Fellows' leftovers. 'Just let them put another half a foot wrong and we'll get them. They deliberately pointed those at the Library, you know.'

'Steady, Bursar,' soothed the Dean. 'Plenty time yet. They're just starting, you know, and God knows how much that little Miss Tanner has put away already. She's bound to throw up somewhere useful in due course. And just wait for the *Monks* to arrive.' He cackled in anticipation.

The first glass had been downed and the second was being filled as Big Jo warned of an important agenda and that this was the only College society which knew how to operate important business. Moving over to her wardrobe she pulled out an ancient, green-coloured gown and took her place at the head of the table. 'You will doubtless recognise this one,' she observed. 'Anyone raise that?'

Gasps of appreciation were followed by silence. They did not quite hear the bellow of rage from the other side of the quad.

'Well,' cooed Jo, 'agenda!'

Minutes of the last meeting were approved, brief reports made of recent conquests, the traditional item of clothing displayed as evidence, congratulations were expressed all round.

'Excellent progress, fellow *Virgins*,' commented Jo. 'Please record in the Minutes my personal sense of satisfaction at the highest of standards being maintained in this, the most distinguished of all College societies. I say this because the next item on our agenda concerns the election of two members to replace those who are already on their way to screaming brats and a mortgage.' Smirking all round.

'Their names are before us and we must proceed to interview. First, though, does anyone feel these candidates do not possess the necessary qualities to join us?'

Uneasy silence. Some shuffling on seats.

'Very well,' said Jo in her most business-like tone. 'Call the first!'

Sarah went to the door and beckoned to Nellie Hughes. Swaggering in on her exceptionally high heels, Nellie made an impressive sight. Everything was tight and glittering.

'Ye Gods,' barked the Dean, 'it's that first year historian whose father's an MP. Blast! But what an outfit.' He adjusted his binoculars.

'Sit down,' said the Bursar. 'Plenty lolly there. She'll pay the fine double quick to avoid any scandal. This could be a good evening.'

'Please sit down, Miss Hughes,' said Big Jo, motioning Nellie to the end of the table, where a bottle of Bollinger was waiting beside two glasses. 'Would you like to join us in a modest drink?'

Nellie had been well primed. 'Thank you,' she said gracefully, and began unwinding the wire on the cork. 'Where would you like it shot?'

'Library, of course,' snapped Jo, worried that Nellie was playing it a bit too coolly and it would all appear a prepared show.

'Of course,' said Nellie. 'Apologies.'

That was better. Jo smiled. The cork gave an excellent bang and whistled in the appropriate direction. So far, so excellent.

'Now then,' said Jo. 'You have been nominated for election to the most prestigious society in St Badley's. What makes you think you deserve such an honour in your very first term here?'

'Well,' said Nellie, 'I'd like to feel I've made a good start. Two on my first night in College, Captain of Boats from St John's, Captain of the Second XV here, and then a member of *The Parsons* from Pembroke. Pinched the Chaplain's gown for formal hall last week. Oh, and I got fined by the Bursar for drunk and indecent after the freshers' dinner.'

'Good start indeed,' conceded Jo. 'Any questions from other members? You are, after all, only in your fourth week, so you must not be disappointed if you need to prove consistency'.'

'Of course,' smiled the well-primed Miss Hughes. 'I should be honoured to join at any point.'

There being no questions, Nellie left for the others to come to a decision. There was some dissent from Sly Susie, a voracious modern linguist whose appetites could, she claimed, only be satisfied abroad, but there was no doubt that Nellie was showing immense promise and probably needed to be encouraged. She was called back in and given the good news.

'I am deeply honoured to join you,' she proudly proclaimed. 'And I promise to bring nothing but glory to

The Virgins.'

'I am delighted to welcome you,' said Jo. 'You know the rules: they are quite simple and undemanding. An average of one man a week in term, never lose an opportunity to flirt with any Senior Member, and, above all, never associate with anyone from that appalling College next door to our own.

'Now, as Junior Member, would you be so kind as to call in the next applicant?'

Nellie went to the door and, with a sense of disdain, curled her finger at Catherine Hayter.

There was no doubt that Catherine had tried hard. She'd bought the first mini-skirt of her life, she looked dreadfully uncomfortable in a bra which didn't do as much for her cleavage as it had undoubtedly claimed, and she was having grave difficulty with her stilettos. How she had managed her qualifying exploit was quite beyond the grasp of all who knew her.

'Now then, Miss Hayter,' said Jo in her most encouraging voice. 'What makes you think you are worthy of joining our illustrious group?'

It had taken some time for Bursar and Dean to recognise the new face. Now that they had, they were taken aback. The Dean suddenly drew himself up in his chair. 'Bursar,' he declared, voice almost trembling. 'You know what this probably means, don't you?'

'Er... remind me.'

'We both know the rules for joining this appalling society, but there is one magic route which means that however few you've had, you still get in.'

'Er... enlighten me.'

'Experience with a Fellow!' exploded the Dean. 'Disgraceful! Disgusting! Who on earth can it have been? Because I have no doubt that wretch of a classicist – whom I myself have taught for Ancient History – can't have any other claim for membership!'

Catherine was having difficulty in her chair. She hadn't dared to pour herself a glass of champagne and she was wondering whether her three-year wait had been worth it.

'Well,' she began, and then remembered she had been trained never to start a sentence with that word, so she launched immediately into her prepared speech.

'I must confess my experience is probably a bit more restricted than that of other members of the society.'

Smiles all round.

'As you know, I am in my fourth year now, and I've had to put most of my efforts into work in order to get on the Masters course. But now that I've made it, I'm about to change, and I have... been... er... I've slept with a Fellow *five* times since the beginning of term.'

Sly Susie felt so sorry for Catherine she pushed another bottle in her direction. Catherine took the hint but poured badly; too much found its way onto the cloth and the floor; she then sneezed loudly as the bubbles got up her nose.

'Any questions?' demanded Jo of the others. 'No? Well, would you kindly wait outside, Miss Hayter. As you know, your case must be discussed in full.'

Catherine swayed towards the door. No one was sure whether she'd rush away before the decision was reached. And no one was quite clear why she wanted to join either. Was there really a quivering body beneath that demure exterior?

'Hard one to call,' commented Jo gently. 'Any views?'

'Poor thing,' said Softie Susie, who had a weak spot for her own sex. 'Did you see her stockings? They were hold-ups and she'd put them on a suspender belt! I know the rules, and I suppose we've got to stick with them about admission, but she won't last a term, will she?'

'It's pathetic,' agreed Blondi, 'poor thing's been desperate ever since I've known her – not that I really know her,' she quickly added, 'but rules is rules. Yes,' she repeated with a surprising firmness, '*rules is rules*'.

'Who on earth was the unlucky man?' asked Nellie, a little forwardly for her first meeting.

'That weed of a German astronomer,' explained Jo. 'It's all kosher. I've checked it out. But, as the Vice-President has rightly observed, "rules is rules". We have no choice. My only hope is that membership of the Society will so enhance her standing that she will never be short again.'

Murmurs of approval gave Jo what she needed. 'Very well, then, I think we probably have to vote just to preserve tradition: those in favour? Thank you. Nellie, will you kindly summon back Miss... er... Catherine.'

The clock chimed ten thirty as the newest member of the society, unable to suppress the biggest grin of her life, re-entered and was given a gentle embrace by Big Jo.

'We have exactly thirty minutes before the *Monks* arrive,' announced Jo, 'unless, of course, there is any other business apart from the date of the next meeting, traditionally the final Saturday of term...when we must elect... or re-elect... our President...'

'Yes, there is another matter,' said Blondi, a little gruffly. 'I am afraid it has come to my attention that one of our members has broken our most important rule. And I have no alternative but to name her.'

Jo looked daggers. Damn! It had been well on its way to being the predicted dream and now that wretched bitch of a Blondi was out to ruin it and spoil Jo's chance of re-election. But she quickly realised her role and raised her hands for silence among the excited, whispering band. 'I see,' she said. 'Well... in that case... enlighten us...'

Chapter Two

On the other side of town Peter Thistlethwaite, first year classicist, was emerging from his first meeting of the Modern Theology Society. He'd been taken along by Jane Hart, third year lawyer, whom he'd met in the Chapel choir.

'Thank you very much for introducing me, Jane,' he said, 'I'd no idea Modern Theology was quite so broad-minded. I enjoyed that bit about choices in modern living – especially that idea, bit silly though it was, about a girl keeping hold of a man's hand even though she knew he was after something, but she wouldn't make the choice and rebuff him.' He smiled at having been able to use that example, because he was wondering what Jane might do if he were to take her hand at some point that evening.

'Yes, it was good,' commented Jane, 'but nowhere near as good as the talk we had last term on existentialism and the whole idea of our being what we are only through the eyes of others. That's Sartre too, you know.'

'No, I didn't know that', said Peter, a bit too honestly, since he was anxious to impress Jane, whom he was now determined to give a good night peck on the cheek when they parted. 'Er… can you tell me a bit more?'

'Absolutely,' said Jane enthusiastically. 'Now, just imagine that you found yourself in hell. What would you miss most? Let's say it was a mirror, so you couldn't see yourself. That would be hell to some people. They could only see themselves through the eyes of others.'

'Gosh,' said Peter. 'That reminds me of an awful play I once saw, French author I think it was, which had something like that in it. But the way you put it is so much clearer,' he quickly added. 'Tell me more!'

But before Jane could do so they had to start thinking of some evading action – what looked like a pack of fifteen very large young men was swaying towards them and beginning to wolf-whistle Jane, much to her and

Peter's alarm.

'You should be in bed at this time of night!' howled one of them, an observation which brought most of the rest to a guffawing standstill. Peter, much to his own surprise and satisfaction, took Jane's hand protectively and pulled her firmly over to the other pavement. They moved on more swiftly towards St Badley's, their philosophical discussions temporarily interrupted while they commented on the state of morals in Oxford.

'There is a terrible woman in the room below me,' noted Peter, 'she's often drunk and there are always men flitting in and out. I asked for the cheapest room in College, and now I know why I got it. And the noise from the bar is terrible. I'm on the staircase just next to it. I'd no idea people got drunk so often.'

'Perhaps you should see my room,' suggested Jane sweetly. 'It's a scholar's room, so it's quiet and it's got a lovely view of the side of the Library.'

'I'd love to see it,' said Peter hopefully, wondering whether this was the way mature women enticed you into their dens. If this was a genuine invitation, then his offer of a 'quick half' in the bar wouldn't be necessary. He trembled with excitement. They were half-way back now. And Jane hadn't removed her hand from his. This was the life! 'Um... tell me more about that seeing yourself as others see you.' He grinned at how cleverly he had grasped it.

'Oh, nicely put!' said Jane. 'Well, it's linked with what's called "bad faith", you know... '

Back at St Badley's, the *Virgins* were also about to engage in serious discussion. Blondilocks was set to mount her case.

'Well...' said she. 'It was brought to my attention that Frankie has been seeing quite a lot of a man from the place next door, and so I had no choice but to check it out. I did. There is no doubt that she has. Far more than once. Rules is rules. She must leave.'

Pandemonium. Frankie turned bright red and blew her nose. Jo was cursing inwardly. It would have to be Frankie, whom everyone liked, was a bit too honest for her own good and who still hadn't quite grasped the concept of the 'one night stand'.

'Frankie,' said Jo in her hardest voice. 'Is it true?'

'Yes,' sobbed Frankie. 'I'm terribly sorry. But I didn't know he was next door… until…'

'We must preserve the rules *and tradition*s of this society' snapped Blondi. 'I move that she leaves.'

Jo pulled the Dean's gown up over her shoulders. Damn bloody B! She was making certain she got her presidency. But what if… She recalled various meetings with the Fellows she'd had to attend in her role as Junior Representative and suddenly it all become clear. She drew herself up in her chair, making full use of her height and bust to show who was in charge. If B wanted a battle, there was nothing for her, Jo, to lose.

'As the Vice-President has so forcefully put it for the second time tonight' she launched out, "rules is rules". But let us not forget that we are a progressive society in a backward college. We must not hold slavishly to the past if modification and adaptation are important to heightening our success.'

Jo paused, grateful she had gained something from those boring meetings in which the Dean and Bursar tried to outbid one another in words which they consistently failed to implement. 'We must reflect on possible alternative measures.'

'I'll do anything to stay' pleaded Frankie. 'Honest, I had no idea of who he was when it started. And he is in the University First Boat…'

Rocky, Captain of St Badley's First Women's Eight, sat up straight. Well, that was one clear vote, thought Jo. Plus tonight's two entrants, surely… Softie Susie wouldn't vote against. Sly Susie was unpredictable, but with Jo's own vote, and Frankie not able to join in… Jo's maths were slow but reliable… she would almost be there! No need to rush it, though, but what on earth could Frankie be made to do as some form of atonement? Ah yes, she had a stunner!

'I am listening for alternative forms of punishment,' said Jo, 'and the obvious one is… no man for the rest of term'.

'Oooh, nasty!' said Sly Susie.

Confirmed, breathed Jo.

'Wicked!' said Liz.

Another vote.

'A dreadful punishment!' agreed Catherine smugly.

Blondilocks looked dejected. She had to win back her position quickly. She cleared her throat.

'As our President has so succinctly put it, we are a progressive society in a backward College. I accept her proposal of an alternative punishment. But how can we possibly monitor Frankie's private life? She has deceived us once. She may do so again.'

Blondi was doing well, but she hadn't a clue how she was going to end up. And over the other side of the quad the Bursar and the Dean were puzzling. There was obviously big trouble. Had the group decided to abandon the traditional romp with the *Monks*? Disaster!

'No,' said Blondi. 'There must be some form of… public humiliation.'

'Hmmm,' purred Sly Susie. 'Ten licks all round?' No one was quite sure which way round the licks might be, but there was clear interest in some quarters.

'Or,' said S.S., one of whose topics was eighteenth-century French literature, 'how about a bit of discipline in front of the society? And a bit of bondage too? Why, in de Sade's *Justine* the heroine is taught a jolly good lesson by…

'Er, no,' interrupted Jo, looking a bit concerned. 'That would…er… hardly be in the spirit of our society, would it?'

Sly Susie looked like someone who has just lost a favourite treat and started biting her nails, much to Jo's disgust.

'Well, what about a bit of good old-fashioned hand-spanking then?'

It was becoming increasingly obvious how Sly Susie got her kicks, but from Jo's frown it was equally obvious what she thought of them.

Just then Softie Susie suddenly broke into an enormous grin. 'Hey', she said, 'I've got it! How about something like… in front of the society with… the weediest man in College? That would be more in our tradition, wouldn't it!'

Ooh, a bit daring, but not bad! In fact, brilliant! And confirmed by titters of appreciation! Jo had won! Frankie would stay, her vote would be there in future and this might be quite a coup for the society when word got round College about breaking of rules. As long as Frankie was drunk enough not to care… and she'd downed another two glasses during the last five minutes…

'I am grateful to the Vice-President for her thoughtful suggestion – and for Susie's… inspired proposal', pronounced Jo. 'Shall we vote on that? All in favour? Thank you. Well, I am sorry about this, Frankie, but let's get it out of the way as soon as possible. And I'm sure you can wear a blindfold if you wish… Now then… where do we find a nice weedy man?'

'The weediest in College' insisted Blondi. 'And I know just who it should be: that repellent swot in the room above. He's probably in bed already. Why don't we take her up there?'

'Oh, God,' said Frankie. 'Him! I really don't think I could do it. Ugh!'

'Rules is rules', snapped Blondi. 'And, Madame President, was not our vote unanimous?'

'Yes,' said Jo. 'Sorry, Frankie.'

Peter and Jane were entering St B's as the clock struck three-quarters.

'Gosh,' said Peter. Jane had not repeated her offer of a

room visit. 'It's late. Er... would you like a... quick half?'

'Hmm, that would be lovely, but... the bar will be packed.'

Still no mention of room visit.

'Well,' said Peter, 'I have a bottle of College sherry in my room. I haven't tried it yet. Would you like a glass?'

Jane hesitated. It wasn't as if she was splurging her virginity on this creature, after all, and he did seem to think highly of her mind.

'Well, just a quick one.'

'This way,' said Peter, feeling very excited. A woman in his room in his first term! And a scholar! Help! They would be kissing next! 'This way,' he repeated.

'What about the *Monks*?' wailed Frankie. 'I'm not doing it in front of them. And they're due any minute!'

'True,' said Jo, 'but they're always late. At least ten minutes, maybe fifteen. Look. I have an idea. Our two new entrants will stay here to receive them. They've never been in on any joint session before, so in a sense they shouldn't be in on this one. They will greet the *Monks* and advise them we have urgent business elsewhere. But the *Monks* are not to know what it is. Clear? And I have another idea. That pathetic nerd... what's he called?... is to be blindfolded so he doesn't know who it is. It could be any of us. Right?'

Blondi looked distinctly displeased, but she had to play along to maintain her position. 'We can use my garter for that,' she added generously, 'it's a pretty broad one.'

Frankie had opened another bottle and was putting it away fast. But she too knew she had a position to maintain and to do so with dignity. 'Right,' she announced, suppressing a belch. 'I am ready to submit to the wishes of the society.'

Brilliant, thought Jo. This is the best day of my life! 'Upstairs!' she commanded. 'Hey!' And she burst out laughing. 'What if he's got someone in bed already!'

Even Blondi couldn't help but snigger at such a

preposterous notion. 'If he's got someone there,' she said, 'then Frankie is to be let off!'

And so with all but Frankie in elated mood, they tottered up the stairs towards the garret.

'Where are they going?' cried the Dean. 'This is appalling. This is quite against all traditions of the society. They are a disgrace to the College.'

'Sit down, Dean,' said the Bursar. 'Have you no other claret? These remains of Tuesday are showing distinct signs of age. Undoubtedly from a bottle with a "low shoulder", as we used to put it in the City…Why couldn't you have got some smuggled out of the Master's Lodge? He's entertaining old Mason-Legge, that slob of a major benefactor tonight, so they were having only the best. Anyway, this lot'll be back. They're probably off to the bar to… find someone from another College whom they can debag. Or maybe some girl,' he added wistfully. 'With any luck they'll bring them back to the *Virgins'* room. Why have the two new ones been left there? Hey, isn't that Thistlethwaite in the quad, the chap who's complaining of hardship and can't pay his bill? Who's he with? A woman?'

'Pah!' said the Dean. 'Nonsense. He couldn't pull a woman if he tried. Only thing Thistlethwaite can do is Greek prose. Although he is quite good at that. I hope he doesn't bump into them on their way to the bar, though. He'd get the fright of his life. He lives above the *Virgin-in-Chief*, doesn't he, the cheapest room in College? Hmmm, that's funny. Why has the light gone on in his room when he's not even reached the bottom of the staircase?'

The *Virgins* were not pleased. Apart from Frankie.

'Perhaps he's in the Library?' suggested Rocky. 'Maybe it should happen there?'

'No way,' said Sly Susie. There used to be extra points for doing that, but the Bursar's always prowling. Don't you remember? He caught me there last term after I was

15

challenged at our mid-term meeting. God knows how he knew where we were. Hundred quid in cash there and then or reported to the Master. Bastard.'

'The bar?' suggested Soft Susie, a little hopelessly.

Silence.

Footsteps on the stair. Ah! A weedy voice. 'This way,' it said. 'Funny, I thought I'd shut the door...'

It was hard to say which of the two new arrivals was more shocked. And the *Virgins* too were put out. Their miserable wretch and... Jane Hart! How on earth dare the biggest third-year swot in College get in the way of their mission? But getting rid of her was child's play, surely...

'Hello, sexy,' said Jo, moving forward and grasping Peter firmly by the waist. 'Why have you kept us waiting, you naughty, naughty boy?'

Jane turned and fled down the stairs. She'd been quite looking forward to that sherry and playing with her legs as she had sometimes practised. The bulge in Peter's trousers had not been lost on her, and she'd been having a few wicked thoughts. But those were the *Virgins*, the whole lot of them, and there was no doubt what they wanted from Peter. They must surely have got the wrong room or the wrong man. Or maybe they hadn't? Heavens! Perhaps she had been spared a most horrible ordeal!

'Well, now, handsome' continued Jo, 'how do you fancy a really good time with a very wicked girl?'

Blondi approached, throwing back her curls in her blatant manner; she drew in her breath sharply, turned round to conceal her smile of derision, and motioned to Frankie to get going.

As the door was firmly closed behind him, Peter wasn't sure whether this was going to be the worst night of his life or far and away the best. Superbly arousing scents were all around him and some sort of elastic was being slipped over his head. Someone was fumbling with his trousers, help, they were being pulled right off! He flailed with his arms but suddenly found himself being carried aloft and dropped on his bed. He realised he was terribly excited. As his underpants were pulled roughly down he heard shrieks of delight all round.

'No!'

'Who would have believed it!'

'Well, don't mind if I do!'

'Frankie, put it on!'

'Hey, this was supposed to be a punishment!'

Peter writhed in blissful agony. His tie and shirt had somehow been pulled away, there were those luscious scents all around, something very tight had been put on the most excited part of his body and now someone was firmly astride him. He recalled a disgusting quip he had once heard about if you were being ravished by someone you quite fancied you might as well lie back and enjoy it. But he hadn't thought it was supposed to apply to men. And lying back was hard! He wanted to respond to the wonderful thrusting on top and suddenly found himself thrusting in response. It was fantastic! He tried to open his eyes, but the black elastic in the way allowed him only a glimpse of a large breast threatening to pop out from a miniature lacey bra. Ooh-la-la! He also saw that the curtains weren't drawn! Good job there were only Fellows' rooms opposite. Thank goodness, the Fellows must be long since off home to their beds.

But they weren't, of course, and the Dean and the Bursar were as if nailed to the spot. The Dean wasn't even using his telephoto lens for what could have been superb photos.

'They've obviously got it in for Thistlethwaite,' gasped the Bursar at last. 'Wonder what he's done to deserve this? Who is it on top? Not Mason, is it? Damn. Poor as a churchmouse. On virtually every hardship fund in College. Same as Thistlethwaite,' he recalled. He adjusted his field glasses again. 'Maybe it's Howard. That would be more hopeful. What on earth are they doing now?'

Frankie had done her bit, it had all been rather quick, but she was now being welcomed back into the fold with a bear hug from Jo and handshakes from the rest. But Sly

Susie had gone back to Peter and was playing with him in the way, all assumed, continentals must do it.

'Another!' gulped the Dean. 'This is too much. We must get over there immediately. That's Susie Tanner isn't it? Didn't she cough up fifty quid to you on the spot last term? Why are we still here? *In flagrante delicto*! Worth at least a hundred from each of them! Quick. Put the light on! Where's my gown? Oh, of course! Damn! I'll pick up the Chaplain's on the way. Chapel will be empty, won't it? Unless...' But the thought was too much for the Dean, who clasped his chest to make sure its contents were still under control.

Peter was in eighth heaven. He had stopped trying to understand. He was vaguely trying to see himself as if through someone else's eyes, and he rather liked what he saw. How naïve to think Jane Hart could have been worth his precious sherry! Huh! Stuck-up scholar with weedy legs and absent bosom! What he could see under the elastic was way beyond even the disgracefulnesses he had glimpsed in a magazine left in the Junior Common Room early one Sunday morning. And he was getting so excited again! He involuntarily thrust upwards, to a cheer of encouragement. He shut his eyes firmly and tried to forget that he was supposed to be reading the lesson in Chapel tomorrow. Jane could do it...

But Jane, alas, was not doing quite as well. She'd managed her way down the steps from Peter's garret, but now, blocking her way, were some hungry-looking hulks demanding to know where 'the *Whores*' were. The Monks were early. They had had a poor night so far. Three of their number were out of action due to a rather heavy session the previous evening. They had been unable to take over their own College bar, and now they were being told that the *Virgins* were off on 'urgent business'. And one of the new admissions to the club was a distinctly miserable-looking creature! How the hell had she got in?

This was a bit of an anti-climax to the 'better than usual' tossing for partners that Big Jo had promised. And being fobbed off with an obvious lie that the *Virgins* were 'upstairs' was now made worse by Jane Hart coming down to greet them. Who the hell was this *second* ugly specimen! Gross! What on earth was happening to the best society in Oxford? They managed a half-hearted 'strip! strip!' before they thought better of it and wondered which of them might score Nellie, about whom there was no hesitation whatsoever. But there was only one Nellie and quite a few of them.

'Give's a kiss, then,' said one, now past caring and drunkenly lurching towards Jane. But he held back as he heard footsteps bounding up the stairs. The *Monks* glanced over their shoulders in anticipation. Ah, that sounded hopeful! But as Bursar and Dean sailed past them, they realised the early evening punch had clearly been stronger than even they had imagined. One of them simply sat down and the others slowly, puzzledly, drifted off back towards the bar.

And now it was time for Bursar and Dean to find their version of heaven. With the Chaplain's large gown fitting badly over his feeble frame, the Dean drew himself up and marched boldly in to the 'debauchery on a scale never before witnessed in this college! Shameful, unbelievable behaviour befitting animals of the most primitive nature! Events likely to shock the nation were they to be revealed, and which merited the most severe of punishments which the Bursar had no choice but to exercise in his absolute discretion.'

Jo was close to collapse. The dream had again evaporated. What on earth was going on tonight? This really had put paid to a third term as President. Damn! Or, on the other hand…

'Bursar,' she said authoritatively. 'Please come down to my room and I shall be pleased to pay any fine on behalf of my friends who have got a little carried away this evening.'

Silence.

'Cash?' asked the Bursar.

'Of course,' said Jo.

'Well, said the Bursar, in that case... but I count eight of you. You have eight hundred in cash?'

Jo swallowed. Oh, well, it was quite a bit less than a month's allowance, and she'd get something back from Soft S, for sure. And it would definitely confirm her Presidency. Definitely.

'Of course. Four hundred now and the rest first thing tomorrow morning.'

'That's my gown, isn't it?' said the Dean.

'Please follow me,' said Jo.

The Bursar fell in immediately while the Dean surveyed the room. With difficulty he dragged his eyes off the still semi-naked Frankie, dressed only in her bra, blue stockings, and suspender belt, and tried to find something to calm his pounding heart. His eyes fell on the exposed Peter, who was somehow hoping he might be overlooked.

'Thistlethwaite!'

Peter shot bolt upright.

'Sir?'

'Do you have one hundred pounds, cash?'

'No, sir.'

'Report to the Master at 9.15 tomorrow morning. You are guilty of gross moral turpitude. And may God have mercy on your soul.'

'Yes, sir,' said Peter.

Jane would definitely have to read that lesson in chapel now.

Chapter Three

Sir Richard Mason-Legge had had a good night. He always did when he was eating and drinking at others' expense, even though he could comfortably afford the best cuisine in England. But earlier, and sometimes more difficult, years had fostered in him that pleasant glow of enjoying 'something for nothing' whenever others were paying, and he had certainly had a hellovalot for nothing last night! Not to mention being fawned on by the Master of his old College, a juicy bonus. How could that man be so stupid as to imagine the next benefaction was coming out of his own pocket! The firm needed to set more than ever before against its profits, and putting something into education was bound to go down well in his bid for a Lordship.

Mason-Legge cackled to himself as a reluctant Butler knocked on his door with a substantial breakfast and – God bless the foresight of the Master – *two* discreetly concealed packets of Alka-Seltzer. What time was he supposed to say farewell this morning? 9.15? Time for a few deals before then… Munching away on the sausages, he looked round for his mobile phone. Struggling with its tiny keys, far too small for his massive fingers, he got through to the office and had himself brought up to date on market sentiment.

Peter Thistlethwaite, by contrast, had had an awful night. Paradise had evaporated abruptly with the arrival of Authority, and he was now dreading the worst from the Master. Surely they couldn't send him down? Not in this day and age? But what if they did? What would his father, the vicar, say? And his mother, the vicar's wife? And his uncle, reputedly close to a bishopric? And how was he going to face Jane Hart? He made a cup of coffee and reflected on those wonderful, crazy ten minutes. The more he thought, the more he realised his side of the story was simply incredible. Should he simply leave College now? Nine o'clock. Quarter of an hour to go.

The Master was not pleased by the arrival of both Dean and Bursar. Both his head and stomach were in need of attention, and the kitchens were claiming that they had given away their last Alka-Seltzer on his very instructions. He'd tried to keep pace with the insatiable Mason-Legge, and now he was regretting it. Not least because the old bounder hadn't yet said how much he was coughing up this time. He needed to be on top form for their meeting at 9.30. Why couldn't these stupid Deans and Bursars sort out their own bloody problems?

'Make it quick,' he said. 'I have a very important meeting with a major benefactor and I shall blame you if I am not in the right state for it.'

'Oh, Master,' bleated the Dean, 'we all know your brilliant capacity for handling these benefactors, indeed, that was one of the main reasons for your election! This is, by contrast a very trivial matter, but the Bursar and I have no choice but to approach you, since we fear a first-year needs to be sent down for gross moral turpitude.'

'What!' said the Master. 'We must keep this quiet. I don't want Mason-Legge getting a whiff of it. What has the miscreant done?'

'Master,' took over the Bursar, 'as a man of the world and a former distinguished name in the City, ever since I agreed to control the accounts of this College I have tried hard to ensure that all women here are treated with respect and dignity. Just as they are in the City. Coming back from the Library last night, where the Dean and I had been checking a reference to resolve a disagreement on a particular line in Ovid, we recalled that the College society "The Bluestockings", an intellectual gathering for women only, were holding a meeting. We glanced up at the room in which this was taking place to find there had been an invasion by a man, who, at the window and in full view of the College, was… decency forbids me to go on, but when we entered the room in question there was little doubt that this morally depraved monster was about to perform the same act on every member of this timid and frightened group. There was no doubt that the women in question had allowed him in, that was foolish and they have been fined fifty pounds for it. But the man... The Dean and I are convinced we have no choice but to recommend his being sent down in order to set an example to other undergraduates, who will see they need to pay any... who will see that everyone must pay the *full* price for appalling behaviour. Heavens knows what wild fantasies he will come up with, but we rely on your wisdom and discretion to deal with him immediately.'

'Indeed,' purred the Dean. 'There is in addition every chance of his failing his exams – I fear his Greek prose makes me shudder – and he...'

'Is he or his father a potential benefactor?' demanded the Master.

'I have checked this morning,' reassured the Bursar, 'and discover the man has already plundered every hardship fund in College. His father is a vicar, and I suspect the man himself will in due course change to Theology. This is a figure of whom we are well rid.'

'Right,' said the Master. 'Send him in right away.'

'He is due at 9.15.'

'What! Get him here as quickly as possible! I don't want him in the way of Mason-Legge.'

'I shall deliver him immediately,' said the Dean. 'I wondered whether in addition to being sent down he should make an apology to "The Bluestockings", but perhaps we should spare them further distress.'

'Get on with it!' shrieked the Master. 'Immediately!'

The Dean and the Bursar scuttled out.

Peter had decided there was no point in being late and that he might as well sit on the Master's fine sofa than on his own hard chair. So he missed the Dean, who was nevertheless relieved to find his gown neatly folded on Peter's bed. He put it on immediately and set off for the obvious place, the Library. Peter let himself be ushered into the drawing room by the Master's petite secretary, who regarded him with a sense of awe Peter found a little disconcerting. He had barely begun to enjoy the soft pleasures of the legendary sofa when a burly, besuited figure strode purposefully in.

'Is there a queue?' guffawed a large mouth. 'Someone else come to give the College a million?'

Peter stood up. This man obviously deserved respect of some sort.

'Alas, no, sir,' he admitted. 'Indeed, if I had had a mere hundred pounds I might not be here now.'

'Eh?' said the figure. 'What you here for then?' His mobile phone rang.

'Yeah? Yeah. No. Yeah. Sell. Yeah, the lot. Now then, young fella, what you here for?'

'Er…er…'

'Out with it, man!'

'Gross moral turpitude, sir. But…'

'You're not! Well I'll be blowed! They tried to send me down for that once! Stand your ground, man! Bribe 'em!' He was glowing. 'Knowing this lot, shouldn't take more than half a grand!' He had grown in stature and was gesticulating wildly when another figure entered the room.

'Ah, Sir Richard!' cooed the Master. 'I am so very sorry. I had no idea you were here already. What punctuality! I regret you have been kept waiting a second, especially in the presence of… an undergraduate…'

'Is it true?' bellowed Sir Richard triumphantly. 'Gross moral turpitude! What? Where? When? How?'

'Oh, Sir Richard, do come into my study, I have a splendid little "hair of the dog" for us both…' and with that the guest was steered into the adjacent room.

'Now then,' said Mason-Legge, 'I want to know! Gross moral turpitude! Wonderful! With a girl? Bloke? Dog? Front quad? Library? Hohoho!'

'Sir Richard, Sir Richard, please, please, a most

unfortunate – and, I hasten to add, most untypical, indeed, unprecedented episode – with the women's intellectual society, "The Bluestockings", I believe, for which the wretched man will pay with his place here…'

'Blue stockings? Just can't find a woman with stockings nowadays, you know, hopeless, love 'em myself, reminds me of my wasted youth, what did you say about unprecedented, hohoho, how many bluestockings are there?'

'Eight, I believe, but the…

'Eight! No! That little squirt out there? Really? Wow! Well, well, well…' His phone rang.

'Yeah? Yeah. No. What? No! No! Oh, shit! On my way.' And with that he breezed past the Master into the drawing room. He had almost reached the far door when he swung round. Feeling in his pocket he pulled out a card and thrust it into Peter's quivering hand.

'If you ever need a job, young fella, you get in touch with me. Eight! Take my hat off to you!'

And with a nostalgic glint in his eye, he marched briskly from the room.

'Thistlethwaite!' Mason-Legge might have gone, but the Master hadn't. His face was as black as thunder. 'Come into my study.'

Trembling, Peter entered the sanctum.

'Thistlethwaite, you are a vile, disgusting excrescence. Do you have a million pounds? No, of course not. Do you', he added in a slightly softer voice, 'have a thousand? No, of course not. You are a blight on this distinguished and forward-looking College which can only reach its true heights without corrupt-minded vulgarities such as yourself. I am sending you down forthwith. Do not let me set eyes on you again. Get out!'

'Yes, sir', said Peter. 'Thank you, sir.'

Chapter Four

Peter's departure from St Badley's had been relatively swift. With gleeful disgust the Head Porter had told him he had to be out by evening. An attempt to talk to Jane had been brought to a painful close with the suggestion that a letter of abject apology might be preferable, and a phone call to his cousin, a student of economics in London, had brought nothing more than the half-hearted offer of a 'floor for the night'. Peter caught the 4 o'clock train and hit the capital's rush hour perfectly. Clasping his two heavy bags, he turned up in Kentish Town at 7, to be greeted by a cousin who was remarkably curious to know the reasons for being sent down nowadays. Peter gave him a slightly censored version of the story, ending with the card from Mason-Legge. His cousin looked at it in amazement.

'Effing 'ell,' he said. 'You know who this is? One of those who move markets. *What* did you say he said to you? If you could get in there, you'd be made.'

'I'm not sure whether I'd like to work for him,' said Peter. 'Awfully brash.'

'That's precisely how markets are moved,' said his cousin with a sense of authority. 'I'd give anything for a job there. You sure he made you an offer? Hey, you could get me some hot tips! Dad gets them sometimes, but they're a bit stale by the time they reach me. Go for it, mate!'

'Not much choice, have I?' said Peter. 'How long can I use your floor?'

Mason-Legge plc, with offices in Paris and Frankfurt, had its headquarters in Bishopsgate. Peter marvelled at the bright glass, the smart young men and women in suits, the sense of glamour, urgency, success. He had coffee at a tiny stall nearby and was horrified at the price. The commissionaire in front of the building had grandly waved him past, and the receptionist on the ground floor had also beamed happily when he showed the cherished card. But the sixth floor was more demanding, and the card held little sway here.

'So the Chairman and CEO offered you a job, did he?' leered an unconvinced and dragon-like woman. 'And what sort of a job might that be? Messenger boy?'

Peter was about to abandon the enterprise when the dragon suddenly paused and her eye began to twinkle. Peter could tell someone Very Important was approaching him from behind. He tried to work out the speech to come: 'Sir, this worm has dared not only to mention your name, but to actually suggest you offered him a job!' He looked round.

'Ah!' roared Mason-Legge. 'Turpitude itself! Hohoho! Come for a job, have you? Barbara,' he turned to the dragon, 'send this man off for psychological testing immediately. It is the day for our tame trick cyclist, isn't it? Still, I'm buggered if I'll listen to a word he'll say: this man's likely to go far.'

And then he added, a touch seriously, 'but we mustn't let him go too far... in fact,' he corrected himself, 'we'd better keep a pretty good eye on him!' And, in a much more secretive and deferential voice, '*Eight in one night!*'

Within half an hour Peter was with the psychologist, who totally failed to match expectations. He was very far from being a little man with a thick Viennese accent and a floppy bow tie. He was big, strong, and handsome. He knew where he was going. He had an exceptionally smart suit, a rather flamboyant tie, and a very neat beard. He looked as if he should have had a glass of champagne in his hand. He was completely unlike anything Peter had encountered at St Badley's.

'Just a few standard questions to start off,' he said casually. 'The sort of thing people in my line of business have to ask, although I'm not what you might call... orthodox. I'm here to support people with problems in their work – high stress business this trading, you know – and I'm here if you need to need a bit of counselling. But I also have to assess hopefuls before they start. We wouldn't want to employ you if you weren't quite right for the job, would we?'

What a breath of fresh air, thought Peter. What a nice man!

'Of course not. Thank you, sir,' said Peter, 'that is very kind. Ask whatever you like.'

'OK,' said the psychologist, smilingly benignly, 'Ever fancied your father?'

'What!' exclaimed Peter. 'But...but... what did you say??'

'Interesting response!' came the reply, 'and your reaction tells me a good deal... But,' he sighed, 'let's get more traditional. Life is never easy. Ever fancied your mother?'

'Why, good lord no... er... you haven't met my mother...' he smiled.

'That's what they all say!' said the psychologist triumphantly. 'And quite a different response to the way in which you fancied your father! Hohoho! Never heard of Oedipus, have you?'

'Well of course I have,' countered Peter, slightly affronted, 'classical tragedy by Sophocles in which poor Oedipus actually marries his mother by accident...'

'By accident! By accident! What a load of bullshit! Fancied her from the start he did, so he bumped off his father and bingo!'

'But sir...'

'But bollocks! Are you saying Freud got it wrong? Impossible! If I gave you an envelope and told you never to open it because it contained a secret about your mother, how long would you wait before you opened it?'

'I wouldn't, sir.'

'Wouldn't open it or wouldn't wait? Hohoho! Now, then, let's get serious. How unhappy was your childhood?

'Er... I had quite a happy childhood, sir.'

'Oh come on! How often did you hear your parents on the job?'

'What!… Er… I don't think they ever did.'

'Oh, fuck me! Are you deaf?'

'Pardon?'

'Hohoho! Nice one! What do you dream about most, apart from women?'

'I don't have many dreams, sir.'

'Jesus wept! You choose to repress them! Can you remember anything with a train in it? Or a mineshaft? Or a ferret?

'A ferret??'

'Ahah! Now we're getting somewhere! Blondes or brunettes?'

'Blondes or brunettes what, sir?'

'B' me, you're a tough one! What's the earliest memory you have of a woman with golden hair?'

'I suppose it must have been the Virgin Mary in the big stained glass window in my father's church.'

'My sweet god! What a find! Why the hell didn't you say your father was a vicar?

'But you never asked me.'

'Repressed! Repressed! Ah, it's all falling into perfect shape! Now then, how about this: What's a "straddle"?'

'Sorry, sir, I've no idea. I suppose it's something sexual..?'

'Brilliant!' said the psycho. Confirms all I thought! I was actually referring to a basic concept in the stock market! Now then, what's a "PE"?'

'Sorry. I suppose it's got nothing to do with Physical Education..?'

'Absolutely nothing,' said the ologist, 'but what a great answer! You didn't have a gym mistress rather than a gym master, did you?'

'No sir, certainly not.'

'Quite. Absolutely. Proves my point. Gods, what a classic case! Now then, if you found a tenner on the floor, what would you spend it on?'

'I'd hand it in at the desk, sir.'

'How many times a day do you lie?'

'I never lie, sir.'

'How many women have you slept with?

'One… and a half, I think, sir.'

'One and a half, eh, one and a half…' said the psychologist wistfully, 'nothing like a quick half when you're young! But we've got to get really serious now… Spell 'pervert' backwards. Good. Spell 'sexuality' backwards. Excellent. Here is a list: money, underwear, opportunity cost, bra, insider dealing, knickers, now let me have that backwards. Wow! Phenomenal! OK then, how about this: what's six squared, halved, halved again, squared, now take away the number of steps in a famous novel by John Buchan… Take your time. Wow! Overall absolutely effing amazing. Where did you get that awful suit?'

The psychologist sat back and lit a cigar. 'Well, well, well,' he mused, 'an interesting case. Sex on the brain, that's for sure, you poor beggar. But you're bright! What on earth are you scheduled for? Currencies? Futures?'

'No, sir,' said Peter, 'but I would be happy if I could secure my future with anything.'

The psychologist puffed on his cigar with obvious pleasure. Peter had to admit, it did smell rather good. He suddenly had a longing to try one. Oh dear, what would his father say…

'You know,' said the psychologist, 'even Freud admitted, sometimes a cigar is only a cigar. Magic. Pure magic. Just imagine: a cigar only a cigar! I think that's the one and only occasion he might have got it wrong. But I digress… now then, are you one of M-L's fancy types? He often takes a shine to the most hopeless of the hopeless on a crazy whim and blow me, within a week they're out. I'm supposed to spot the gamblers before they start, but I'm buggered if he listens to a word I say. Never mind. You've got great potential for something, that's for sure. You really only slept with one and half women? And with sex on the brain like you? You poor sod. I'm on a multiple of forty-two tonight. Big occasion. Ah, repression, repression... When do you start here?'

Mason-Legge believed in sink-or-swim. A few words of introduction and then the deep end. But the 'training' made the Dean's classes on Greek prose seem a dream by comparison. All the 'trainers' had distinct touches of the great M-L about them, and they took pride in cultivating the image. None of them seemed troubled by Peter, who responded quickly to everything except their dirty jokes, which he usually didn't understand. Before the week was out, he was really getting the feel for the office. He liked the way he was relied on for his memory of detail. He got excited by the smart little secretaries in their sleek suits and the way they sometimes winked at him. He savoured the buzz when some big deal had gone through and M-L breezed between the desks bellowing congratulations. He loved the way he could stay in the office until long into the night, learning about Tokyo, Hong Kong, Sydney. Everything was more relaxed then, those who were left behind found the time to explain things in full, he began asking the sort of fundamental questions every good classicist wants to but never can, and on Friday he found himself in M-L's office.

'Thistle,' grunted the Big Man. 'Dunno what to make of you. Will always take me hat off to you, that's for sure. Eight in a night! You little bounder! Now, where was I? Ah, yes, no one has quite worked you out but sort of feeling you could fit in somewhere rather well. You've got a damn good memory, if nothing else. *Blue* stockings, wasn't it? Always fancied black fishnet myself. Boring, I know. Can't shake off your youthful fantasies. Now, where was I? Ah yes, going to send you on a course. Special job here at the end of it. OK?'

'Yes sir, thank you, sir. Will I be paid?'

'Paid, *paid*? You not on the payroll yet? Scrooooge!' he bellowed down one of his intercoms, and five seconds later a hunched old man whom Peter had never noticed before came in. 'Scrooge,' said M-L, 'start Thistle on twenty-five. And give him something upfront. Oh, and he'll need a card when he gets back from his course. Oh, and an entertainment card too. Right?'

'Certainly, Sir Richard,' said the Scrooge. 'This way,' he said to Peter.

Peter enjoyed the course immensely. He found himself explaining all the concepts to slower members in the bar at night. He would start the evening with fruit juice and always finish it off with a small sherry. The sherry gave him a special thrill. It reminded him of a night which didn't quite work out the way he had hoped and gave him thoughts of future wickedness. To his concern, he often found himself dreaming of the Virgin Mary getting out of her stained glass window and drifting towards him as she slipped off her cloak. He once woke up in a dreadful sweat when she had almost managed to get her bra off, but he usually woke up well before that point, alas. He was often admonished for wanting to learn rather than to network, but the joys of learning were matched by the thrill of consistently being told he was the best on the course. He had never known anything like this at St Badley's, and he eventually plucked up courage to write to his parents informing them he had left the college, was on a special course, earning £25,000 a year, and hoped to be back in time for Christmas. An irate letter from his father, informing him that his own 'stipend' was only just over twenty and that that sort of money could only be gained by immoral means put paid to the Christmas idea, while his cousin declared that the absence of hot tips meant that his floor was no longer available. So Peter moved into a smart but tiny garret in the City, not much larger than that he had occupied at St Badley's, ten times as expensive, but free of Virgins, Porters, and Deans. And in his cupboard he kept, just in case, a small bottle of sherry.

Chapter Five

Peter loved every aspect of the office. He couldn't quite get into the all-male banter which broke out as soon as none of the women were around, but he smiled appreciatively at every joke, even if he didn't quite understand it, and stored them all up for future use. What if he were some day invited back to the Vicarage and could use even the mildest of them? His mother would faint! He'd thought the City was supposed to be quite politically correct, but maybe it was just this office that was different? He felt very much at home in a male environment, and he was a bit uneasy when he was having to talk with any of the women.

It was already December, and the famous Christmas Party about which he had heard was on its way. It was supposedly one of the best in the City. People were coming from the Paris office too, as well as from nearby brokers. It looked as if parties in the City were not quite what Peter was accustomed to at home: a small glass of sherry on Christmas Eve before Carols by Candlelight in a freezing church. Every year the congregation grew smaller and the church seemed colder. Peter couldn't wait for bed. But not being able to wait for bed seemed to be a concern of the City too.

'Can't wait to get that juicy little blonde on the Far East desk between the sheets,' declaimed one of the analysts, rubbing his hands in eager anticipation.

'Between the sheets!' sneered Cocktail Charlie, whose knowledge of spirits was well known far beyond the office. 'Between the sheets is traditionally one part gin, one cognac, one triple sec and a squeeze, oh yes, a very nice little squeeeeze of lemon juice. But what romantic twaddle. You mean a bang in a broom cupboard!'

'I agree one thousand and one basis points,' declared one of the dealers. 'No taste! Banging the breastless in broom cupboards, I ask you! Now that sophisticated little over-bosomed brunette in European analysis, and in a dark quiet corner, with or without any of Charlie's magic potions…'

Just then a woman appeared in the doorway and the conversation turned immediately to straddles and PEs.

'Who are you after, Peter?' demanded the senior dealer, when the coast was clear. 'I don't want you getting into something unsuitable and ruining your eye for the real thing.'

'Ah well,' said Peter, 'there's a rather nice looking young woman in the back office, but she wears a crucifix rather than a cross, so I'm not so sure…'

'Hey, you don't half like a challenge,' piped up another dealer. 'If you can get *her* knickers down, I'll eat my hat. And if you can prove it… I'll eat *your* hat!'

The Party was scheduled for the Friday night before Christmas. That morning large cases of all sorts of alcohol been stacked up in the office. It didn't look like sherry, that was for sure. M-L spent much time inspecting the labels and trying a glass or two from the odd bottle. Not much work was done that afternoon, but the whole of the City seemed to be away from their trading desks. Peter tried to concentrate on markets where they didn't celebrate Christmas, but they too seemed infected. By mid-afternoon most people seemed to have gone home 'to change'.

'Well, well, well, if it isn't one and a half!'

Peter turned round, a little uneasily. The psychologist was unchanged, except that this time he really did have a glass of champagne in his hand. His beard was even neater. His tie was even more flamboyant. It had a strange design on it, which Peter couldn't quite make out. It looked as if there was some sort of message running down it, starting with the letters 'Bul'.

'Stop trying to read my tie,' said the Psycho. 'It's quite straightforward. It's what makes the grass grow green. Hohoho. Now then, how are you? Still got sex on the brain? Nothing like a grand old love-in for an obsessive like you!'

Just then the girl with the crucifix happened to be passing and smiled.

'Hello', she said, 'I think we're supposed to be mixing. Can I get you a drink? It looks like you've lost your glass.'

'Thank you,' stammered Peter. 'That would be… most kind.'

She'd hardly turned her back when Bullshit grabbed him by the shoulder.

'Keep off, not a hope, you can just see the chains round that bra, she's all a tease, look at that skirt, you can tell, it's an inch above the knee, not a fraction more, but she's tossing it round as if it were half way up her thigh. Nope, don't waste your time! I'll distract her for you, you just go and find someone who's a real goer.'

'But… she's just offered to get me a drink, and, and, her dress is quite low cut as if she's… er she's interested in showing off her breasts – and they're lovely! I'm just not so sure about the crucifix.'

'Eh?' said Psycho. 'What crucifix? Take my word, not a hope. Did you see the way she lowered her eyes when she talked to you? Classic! Femme fatale ungraspable! She's probably called Virginia! Keep off! And what's the bet she comes back with a friend! One she stands out against! I've seen it all before! Keep off!'

Psycho was right. Back she came with a glass in each hand and a slightly mousy looking girl alongside.

'Oh, by the way,' she said, 'I'm Ginny and this is my friend Sarah from the back office'.

Peter wasn't sure what to do. Especially since Ginny couldn't do anything but smile and look… encouraging. Yes, encouraging! But he didn't have the chance to make any decisions, because Psycho clearly had it all worked out.

'You're in the back room,' he said, in a purring voice, staring with admiration at Ginny. 'How underestimated you people are! The dealers and the analysts and all these hangers-on think they run the show, but blow me, without you, they're up that famous creek without a paddle! You're the ones that make it work! Hey, isn't that the Head of the Back Room over there? Let's go and have a chat with him…' And with that, he gently tugged Ginny by the sleeve and pulled her over to the other side of the room.

Peter was nonplussed, but not so Sarah.

'You're supposed to be the next star of the trading floor!' She sighed, looking up at Peter in admiration.

'Oh…er, well, I sometimes do quite well…'

'What's your favourite boy band?'

'Eh? Um… I'm not quite sure.'

'Oh. Who's your favourite pop star at the moment?'

'Er… I… I'm not really into that sort of thing.'

'Oh. What's your favourite night club?'

'I…er… I spend most nights researching…'

'Oh.'

Very awkward silence.

'Oh,' said Sarah suddenly, 'there's two of my pals from the back office over there, must have a quick chat with them…'

Much relieved, Peter sat down and savoured his champagne. It really was splendid. But the occasion itself was rather boring. He seemed to be the only person who wasn't in earnest conversation with someone else.

'Blimey, I just saved you from some awful frustration there,' said the voice which was already a bit too familar. 'I can spot them a mile off. Thank goodness she's gone off to the loo. The crucifix is the key tell-tale. You can see it from the other side of the City. Modern version of a chastity belt. If she took that off, you'd be away, it would be like her taking off her… But she never will. Hey, look at that bit of fluff over there by the door… now that's what you should be after!'

Peter looked over to the door but saw nothing out of the ordinary.

'Which one?' he asked.

'Jesus, are you blind? That one with the short curly hair and the black trousers.'

Peter looked again.

'Er… yes, she's in some aspect of accounts, I think, but... do you really think she's a … goer? She seems as shy as me. Always averts her eyes when I go past her. And if she's got a bosom, she's not particularly keen on showing it.'

'You know,' said the good doctor, 'you would look a gift horse in the mouth. I'm amazed you even managed it one and a half times. But it's written all over her face – there's a really luscious body underneath that very modest outfit, and a sexually vibrant personality to go with it. Boy, if I didn't have something else on my mind at the moment... Go on, go and chat her up! It's the Christmas Party, so you just need to stroll over and say hi, I'm Peter and I've seen you around the place, but I don't know your name. And she'll start crumbling before you – although you won't see it, of course, she'll hide it ever so well. I reckon you need half an hour on her and then she'll melt in your hands. But she'll give the impression of being damn hard to get. Oh yes. Needs time. But well worth it.'

Peter looked towards the door again. The curly haired girl was talking quite animatedly to her female companion, who didn't look much cop either, but since the Crucifix had temporarily disappeared, he decided he might as well have a go. After all, it was the party and they were supposed to be mixing.

'OK,' he said. 'I'll do my best.'

'Attaboy!' said Bullshit. 'Gods, what a cracker!'

Peter strolled over. He wasn't at all confident.

'Hi,' he said. 'I'm Peter. I've seen you around the place, but I don't know your name.'

Curly looked at him with a slightly offended sideways glance.

'I'm Simone.'

'Hi… er… am I right, do you work in accounts?'

'Yes.'

'Ah… must be very interesting there, much better than the boring floor.'

'No, it's pretty dull.'

'Oh. Well, I suppose we do have our odd moments on the floor, especially when M-L has got some bee in his bonnet.'

'I'm sure.'

Peter was getting desperate, but just then Curly's companion broke in.

'You're a trader, are you?'

'Yes,' said Peter, 'it's… sometimes interesting…'

'I've heard you have lots of good trades'

'Well… yes, sometimes I make some pretty good calls.'

'Really?' said the woman, suddenly fluttering her eyelashes and playing with the top button of her blouse.

'Do you… have any good calls at the moment?'

She smiled endearingly at Peter and fluttered her lashes again.

'Warm,' she said, 'isn't it?' Peter thought he could see the top of a pink lacey bra. Oh God!

'Let me get you a drink to cool you down,' said Peter a bit too eagerly. He needed one himself. 'A glass of champagne?'

He glanced at Curly, who was obviously a bit peeved Peter was getting somewhere with her friend! Huh. Served her right! Her pal was much more the real thing. Knew how to respond to conversation for sure. Knew how to get a bloke excited. Oh yes! Curly could learn a lesson or two from her! Curly probably had a plain white bra on. Still, he had to keep her onside for a while.

'Would you like a glass of champagne too, Simone?' Peter managed graciously.

'I've had enough already,' said Simone, rather sharply, 'and so has Kirsty'.

'Oh, I'll just have one more,' said Kirsty, 'and then Peter is going to give me some great tips, isn't he?'

38

'You bet,' said Peter, who was now wondering how he could get rid of Curly, bloody nuisance, getting in the way of his great chatting up lines.

'I'll be back in a tick with your glass – and a great tip!' He promised.

Kirsty fluttered her eyelashes again. Peter suddenly felt very much in control. How the hell could he get rid of surly curly? Silly old bullshit had got her wrong, that was for sure. Or had he been looking at her mate instead? That must be it!

Peter came back with two very full glasses. Kirsty was looking rather flushed. Damn! What was going on?

'Kirsty's decided she's had enough,' said Simone. 'Perhaps you could take her glass back to the bar?'

'Oh…' said Peter. 'Well that's alright, I'll just drink both myself!' But his joke didn't seem to go down well.

'You wanted a tip,' he said to Kirsty, wondering whether he could somehow plant himself between her and her horrible friend.

'Oh yes,' said Kirsty. 'Is it a good one?'

'Damn good,' said Peter, impressed by how well he could use slightly rude words to attractive women. 'Ashington Group. They should soar next week when their interims come out.'

'Thank you,' said Simone, 'very interesting, now Kirsty and I need to be off.'

'Off?' said Peter. 'Oh.'

Simone led the way and Kirsty followed meekly.

Damn! Bloody jealousy, that's what it was. Simone was simply envious that Kirsty had managed to chat him up so well and get his best tip of the month. He watched them go out of the door. He decided to follow, since he needed to get rid of some of the alcohol he'd put away. As he came out of the door and turned towards the gents, he saw them at the end of the corridor, obviously arguing. Huh. He had a good mind to go and grab Kirsty, poor thing, victim of that brute of a so-called friend. And then he saw her suddenly put her arms round Simone and hug her. And then… she started kissing her… Peter froze. Simone started kissing her back. Peter went into the gents in a daze. The alcohol wasn't helping.

As he was drying his hands the Bullshitter came in.

'How are you getting on?' he demanded. 'Don't be disappointed if it seems slow, but the satisfaction of getting someone like her… boy!'

'Boy is not for her,' said Peter firmly. 'She likes girls. That's why she was dressed like that. Couldn't you see?'

'Hohoho!' said Bullshit. 'Nonono! She's obviously bi! I saw it a mile off but didn't like to tell you. Now and again she fancies a bit of her own sex, but what she really wants is a man! Don't you know that the best lays in your life will be with bi's! They see it from both sides! Get back in there!'

'I think I'll have a breath of fresh air first,' said Peter.

'OK,' said B, 'but don't disappoint me! Hey, in the meanwhile, would you like me to introduce you to a really gorgeous bit of stuff who's absolutely gagging for it, and she's taken a bit of a shine to me… but I think I'm…er… a bit old for her, she's much more your age, come on, you'll love her.'

Peter followed reluctantly. Did old B really know what he was talking about? He had dismissed poor sweet Crucifix out of hand, and promised great things of Surly Curly. Well, he'd had multiple of forty-two, however many that might be, and he was a psychologist – or was he really a psychiatrist? – so maybe he knew something. At least he was going to introduce him to someone.

The 'gorgeous bit of stuff' actually lived up to her description. But she was quite a bit older than Peter. She had a very stylish cream dress on, very short, very low cut, hair quite well styled, if a bit ruffled. She had a strange glow about her which was rather attractive, and a happy, self-satisfied smile. She was slumped in a chair, showing off masses of thigh, and almost looking as if she could go to sleep.

'A reviving glass of champagne!' said B, pronouncing 'champagne' in a very French sort of way.

'Ah, chéri, merci!' said the woman, waking up a bit.

Oh, thought Peter. Must be someone from the Paris office. There were supposed to be one or two of them coming over.

'Michelle, ma belle, this is my friend Pierre,' said B. 'He is verrry English.'

The woman looked at Peter and slowly crossed her legs.

'He is supposed to be one of the best traders M-L has seen in years!'

Another slow crossing of the legs. Peter dared look on this occasion. Help! Stockings, mauve suspender belt and a glimpse of mauve underwear!

'You're from Paris?' gasped Peter.

'Ah oui,' said Michelle. 'The city of love and dreams and beauty and... champagne. But Londres... eet is not too bad for love.'

She leaned forward to pick up her glass, revealed an enormous amount at the top, and then curled back comfortably. Heavens, Bullshitter had got this one right for sure! A gorgeous bit of stuff indeed! But how to chat her up?

'Excuse-moi,' said B, 'I've just seen someone on the other side of the room I really must say hello to. Back in under a minute!'

Michelle looked a bit annoyed and recrossed her legs much more rapidly. Nothing on view that time. She looked in the direction B had gone, but he'd completely disappeared. Ah no, there he was deep in conversation with a very stylish looking brunette. And no! Giving her a peck on the cheek! Ooops! A look of enormous disappointment slowly broke over Michelle's face. She sat up straight, took out a handkerchief from her very expensive bag, blew her nose in a very masculine sort of way, got up without revealing anything and strode purposefully off.

She suddenly turned round and glowered at Peter.

'Engleesh is sheet!' she said.

'Eh,' said Peter, very puzzled. 'Sorry?'

'When your friend come back,' said Michelle, 'you tell him he is a sheet-faced dog!' And with that she headed straight for the door.

Peter, dazed once more, sat down. He was immediately joined by the psychiatrist.

'Well done, old man, saved me beautifully there! Here, have a drink,' and he handed over another glass of bubbly.

'I... think you may have upset her a bit,' said Peter.

'Silly Parisian cow. Doesn't understand a bit of a harmless slap and tickle at Christmas,' said B, 'one biggish kiss and she thinks it's permanent! Honestly!'

'Eh?' said Peter. 'You didn't make her any promises... did you?'

'Look,' said his friend, 'there's that girl with the Crucifix again. You know, I think she might be just a little less frigid than I thought! You go and chat her up, that tasty little brunette I'm after has just slipped off to the loo.'

'OK,' said Peter wearily. 'I'll do my best.'

Just then the Number Two dealer came up.

'Hello, Peter,' he said. 'Enjoying the party?'

'Er... well, it's very...um... er not quite what I thought, I er... imagined that people would be sort of circulating and talking to each other, but it looks as if most people seem to be seriously trying to... er...'

'Let's sit down,' said the dealer. 'It's hopeless. Same every year. M-L thinks he's back in the seventies, or maybe the sixties, just wait and see how he starts running the games. We're the most politically incorrect office in the City, you know, and that's saying something. If M-L didn't insist we all came, I'd be long since in bed. Not least since I've got a cold coming on.' And to prove it, he sneezed.

'Bless you!' said Peter, feeling really sorry for Number Two. But he then gawped in disbelief as Two pulled from his pocket a pair of black lacey knickers and drew them across his nose.

Suddenly, obviously feeling a certain roughness and looking slightly horrified, he stuffed them back into his pocket and started searching wildly elsewhere, finally pulling out a large white handkerchief.

'Sorry about that,' he said. He was very red in the face. 'You probably wonder…'

'Yes, I do wonder…' said Peter.

'Well… you'll find out later. M-L sometimes tries to liven things up by starting a scavenger hunt, and this year I wanted to impress rather than coming in last with a handkerchief or nothing at all…'

'Scavenger hunt?' asked Peter. 'Eh? Ah, I see…'

It was gone eleven, and several people had drifted off. Others were clinging to each other rather purposefully. Peter had tried chatting up various people without success and had sat down feeling a bit glum. Just then he was joined by M-L.

'How many you pulled so far, then?' he asked Peter in a low voice. 'I'm having a dreadful evening. Just when I think I'm ready to slip my hand round some nice part of someone's anatomy I get this terrible desire to ease the pressure of nature, and that's the biggest turnoff I know. Gods, I can remember one time when I was just about on fourth base with some smashing bit of crumpet when I just couldn't control myself and it just about made me… well, never mind, and I don't need to tell you what it did to her, so I take jolly good care not to do the same whenever…' he paused and Peter thought he heard a tell-tale noise, 'well, anyway, not when it's work in progress… Hey, this party needs livening up. Now, shall we have a scavenger hunt, or shall we play forfeits? Always good for a giggle. Just make sure you take off the most important bit first…'

M-L got up and clapped his hands. Respectful silence.

'Now then,' he said, 'no party's a party without a party game, so the first one is to be… hide and seek. So… all the women go and hide, and the last one to be found gets a bottle of bubbly to take home!'

Some of the younger women quickly separated from whomever they were with and disappeared. The older ones took their time. Some seemed to be drifting in the direction of the loos. Hmm. Pretty good hiding place.

'Right!' triumphed M-L, 'they think we're going to find them! No, we're going to steal a piece of their clothing, and the person who can steal the most gets a bottle of bubbly! Mind, you, he added, nothing too saucy – yet! And oh yes, let's make it clear who's going to win: it's the man with the most points. And there's five points for a hankie, five for a scarf, five for a necklace, twenty-five for a top, fifty for a skirt, and one hundred for a pair of you-know-whats! Magnum of champagne for the winner!'

Peter was a bit shocked, but just about all the men rushed off in a frenzy and there were soon shrieks of all sorts to be heard. And then the sound of someone's face being slapped. And then an argument, and then a girl without her top came running in crying, and then a man, being hotly pursued by a large young woman. She rugby-tackled him, pinned him to the floor, and roughly removed his trousers, holding them aloft. 'Hey,' she bellowed. 'Does this win the prize?'

M-L looked a bit worried and grasped his own trousers firmly at the waist. Peter hadn't found anyone yet. Where on earth were they?

He started looking under desks at the dark end of the room, and goodness, who had he found!

'Hello, Ginny,' he said in delight. Ginny giggled. 'Oh dear,' she said, 'what do I have to give you to overlook the fact I'm here?'

'Eh?' said Peter. 'Er... er... your... er... necklace?'

'Oh,' said Ginny, clearly a little uneasy. She fumbled with the clasp – Peter wasn't sure whether she was having second thoughts or simply having difficulty – and handed it over with a slightly flushed face..

'Here you are,' she said, 'anything else?'

'Um… er… a handkerchief?' It was out in two seconds.

'Anything else?'

Just then there was a big roar from M-L.

'Time's up! Everyone back for a drink and the prizes!'

Ginny scowled and crawled out from under the desk; she got onto her knees and swayed a bit. Peter lent her a hand to get up.

'Thank you,' she said, giving him a peck on the cheek. 'What a cavalier you are! I've been desperately hoping someone would chat me up properly tonight, and all I've met are people who want to fill me up with champagne as quickly as they can! Especially that bloke with the beard. He really puts on the charm, but honestly, the number of glasses he's made me put away!' She belched slightly. 'Can we have a quiet chat somewhere? But let's sit down, I'm a bit dizzy and I'm not quite sure I know what I'm doing. I don't usually take off my crucifix…'

'Yes, yes,' said Peter. 'But let me just show these to M-L…'

Peter was glowing as he brandished the necklace and the handkerchief.

'What, no stockings?' said M-L in a disappointed voice. 'Quite a few on display. Thought I could have relied on you…'

'The best is yet to be,' said Peter with a big wink. 'The night is young! And look at the necklace – that's what I call a conquest!'

'A cruficix! Begad, what a bounder!' gasped M-L. 'You're a cool one, that's for sure! Why, I remember the first time I ever saw a crucifix underneath me… talk about someone being liberated from inhibitions…'

Peter triumphantly made his way back to Ginny only to find she already had company. Bullshit! Oh, no!

'Hi,' said B, 'I saw you from over the other side of the room and I thought, now *that's* a man who needs a really special concoction! This is a reviver, it'll refresh you no end and put you on top of the world!'

Peter took the blue coloured glass with some reluctance. He sniffed at it. It did smell rather good. He took a sip. Gosh. Bullshit was right: very refreshing. He downed the rest in one go.

'Excuse me,' said Ginny, suddenly, 'I don't feel very well,' and she made a beeline for the Ladies.

'She'll be happier when she's thrown up,' said Bullshit, 'and after half an hour she'll be up for it big time!'

Peter sat down. He himself didn't feel too good.

'I'll just pop off to the Gents myself,' said Psycho. 'See you in a minute.'

Just then Cocktail Charlie turned up.

'Hello, Peter,' he said, 'seen that mad psycho guy anywhere? I just mixed him a really lethal dose that would knock out a horse. Said he was on to something big and needed it to restrain himself! I ask you! Funny bloke. God knows why M-L keeps him around. Anyway, I think I got the ingredients a bit wrong, and he'd better watch himself. Hey, are you alright?

'No,' said Peter, 'I think I need to lie down...'

Some time later, as he looked up from the floor, Peter saw Psycho gently escorting Crucifix from the room. His hand seemed to be round her waist and she was clinging tightly to him. He looked again. That hand didn't just seem to be round her waist, it was right round her bottom! Peter blinked hard. Was he seeing right? And now Psycho was gently tugging at her skirt and she wasn't resisting in the least! And her with a crucifix! He groaned out loud, shut his eyes, and woke several hours later to the sound of someone loudly breaking wind.

'Aaaah, that's better!' he heard a familiar voice grunt in satisfaction. 'Been keeping that in all bloody night!'

With a splitting headache, a raging thirst, a desperate desire for the loo and a sense that the Christmas Party must surely have been good in parts, Peter raised himself up. He suddenly found his trousers were missing and so were his underpants. Someone must have won a big prize…Thank goodness he wasn't due back in the office for a week…

Chapter Six

By February Peter was already taking exams and by March he really felt part of the team. He worked long hours and soon became known for his early morning analysis of Far East trends. He could give the PE of every company in the Footsie without hesitating, and his ideas on straddles were second to none. Everyone wanted him as an assistant. The sleek secretaries started winking at him at bit more often. He realized he definitely preferred the blondes, but he couldn't bring himself to talk to them. He bought a new suit and a range of new ties. He would regularly say 'damn' when the market misbehaved, and he started getting the point of some of the dirty jokes. He was beginning to forget St Badley's until, one morning, dashing out to grab a sandwich for his lunch, he bumped into someone who wasn't in a rush and who was therefore being knocked over by everyone.

'Good lord', said the figure. 'It's... Thistlethwaite, isn't it?

'Heavens,' said Peter... 'You're Paul Challoner, aren't you... you were on the bottom floor of my staircase at St B's! What on earth are you doing here?'

'After a job at Mason-Legge,' said the figure. 'Not very hopeful. Damn hard to get in there. By the way, why did you really disappear in the first term? Did it have anything to do with the Bursar and the Dean getting the sack for financial irregularities? Do you remember Susie Tanner? She got her father on the job after the Dean starting blackmailing some of her friends. There was quite a stink there! Anyway, do you know where the M-L office is?'

'Right through there,' said Peter, suddenly feeling a pang of nostalgia for St B's. 'Oh, by the way, here's my card in case anyone ever asks for me.'

'Ah, Thistle,' boomed the Great Man. 'Doing well, you are. Knew it. A fine taste in stockings never did a man any harm. Too many of my analysts wouldn't know a stocking if they felt one. In fact,' he sighed, 'some of them wouldn't know what a stocking was... Which companies make stockings, by the way?'

Peter named three.

'I'm going to put you on fifty,' said M-L appreciatively. 'And I have a special job for you. Now then, got your account card? We're off to the wine bar.'

'Wine bar?' puzzled Peter. 'But it's only just past eleven o'clock!'

'Precisely,' said M-L. 'Need to do this before twelve. Now, I want you to pay particular attention. I am going to be sarcastic to someone in the bar, right? Make a note of who is with that person, right? You will be seeing that individual every week on Fridays at 11.15. Right? And not a word of this to anyone. Right?'

The Wine Bar was quite unlike anything in Oxford. Bars there were noisy places which Peter barely dared enter, but this establishment hardly deserved that name. Everyone wore a suit. Everyone was drinking wine. Everyone was whispering in the corner seats. The floor was spotless.

'Bottle of Pouilly fumé!' declared Mason-Legge to the barmaid. 'Two glasses!' He brandished his card, signed a piece of paper, and within thirty seconds he and Peter were standing at one of the tables in the middle of the room.

'What are your best memories of St B's?' enquired M-L. 'Apart from the obvious...' he added, in a lower voice.

'Oh,' said Peter, 'I enjoyed textual analysis quite a lot, despite the fact I had to do it with someone from the...er... "shot for shit" brigade.'

'Shot for shit??' guffawed M-L. 'What the hell is that?'

'Well,' said Peter, 'there are some scholars who go round looking at ancient texts and pretending they are much more... er ... dignified than they really are, a bit like Bowdler did with Shakespeare, you know, so when they come across the word "shit" they say it's a transcription error, it should be "shot".'

'I see,' said M-L. 'So if they found... "wank" it would come out as... "wink".'

'Very good!' said Peter. 'You've got it!'

M-L beamed with pleasure. 'Shot for shit, wink for wank... how about fort for fart! Well, well, well. I'll use that some day.'

'These rude words' continued Peter, 'are actually very interesting from a linguistic point of view.'

'*Linguistic* point of view?' exploded M-L. 'Come on, a dirty word's a dirty word, and I bet I know fifty times as many as you do! Let's start with "a"...'

'No, seriously', said Peter in an earnest tone, 'you see, these so-called dirty words are found throughout the world and they are all very short and simple and you can learn a lot about general aspects of a language from them. There used to be a chap in Oxford who specialized in this... he would wait until his lecture audience didn't have any women in it, and then he would launch into an action-packed hour on anything vulgar and how it helped you memorise vowel changes and sound shifts and so on... so in English, for example, "shit" and "fart" could be quite good for showing strong and weak verbs, with shit, shat, shat, but fart, farted, farted... And people remember these...'

M-L was staring at Peter in what seemed to be admiration, but they were interrupted.

'Hello, M-L' said a man who looked like a retired colonel in an old film and had a besuited middle-aged female on either side of him. 'Had any better luck with BZ recently?'

'One of my mistakes' said M-L wistfully. But at least I kicked MCR into touch for a while. Don't try to tinker with my patch, you old oaf. Go back to your... forting!' He laughed heartily.

The Colonel looked slightly puzzled, scowled, and left.

'Was that the...'

'Don't be silly,' said M-L, turning to smile gracefully at a frail, silver-haired man with a stick and a sad-looking young woman beside him.

'How's business today, then?' said the man. 'Got over SCI, have we?'

'Little wobble there,' said M-L. 'Pity about your dabble in telecoms. Stick to what you understand, like… underwear. Or winking!' And he guffawed. 'By the way, anyone moved their team in on you yet?'

'You crook,' said the man under his breath, 'you'll come to a sticky end some day, you wait…' and shuffled off.

'Was that…'

'Shut up and enjoy your drink. Get on, man, I'm three ahead of you. Château de Tracy this one, you know.'

Peter sipped the wine. It seemed awfully sour. He wished he was back in the office.

'Ah,' said M-L suddenly, 'top of the morning to you, Ollie.'

'Ah, Sir Richard! What an incomparable pleasure! Surprised you've managed the time to leave your thriving little business!'

Peter breathed a sigh of relief. That seemed a better start to a conversation. And the newcomer, who looked as if his commands were obeyed fairly quickly, had a rather attractive young woman in tow. Peter smiled at her. She ignored him.

'Ah, we can't be chained to our desks all day!' said M-L. 'How I envy you the time you manage round the City, at the racecourse, at the opera! And now here. A drop of old medicinal, no doubt!'

Peter was puzzled. He'd never heard M-L like this before. Voice restrained, oozing charm. Perhaps they were old army chums?

'No doubt,' said the General. 'Must be on my way. Never a good idea to have too long a drink anywhere near you. The desire to work might get me. Hoho!' And with that he was off.

'Drink up your Pouilly fumé,' said M-L. 'We're back to the office.'

'But aren't you supposed to be being sarcastic to someone?' asked Peter.

M-L stared hopelessly at him.

'Did you see that woman just now?'

'Yes, but…'

'You will meet her here next week. Right? I'll give you a few more instructions on the morning itself.'

Seven days later Peter descended the steps to The Bar, a small envelope in his pocket and some simple instructions imprinted on his brain.

'I'd like a glass of Pouilly fumé, please,' he said meekly to the barmaid, fumbling in his pocket for his wallet.

'Cash?' said the barmaid. 'I don't think I've got any change. Haven't you got a card?'

Peter rarely used his own credit card, but it suddenly dawned on him he had been given something special by Scrooge. With some unease he pulled it out and gingerly put it on the bar.

'Sign here,' said the barmaid. Trembling slightly with a sense of power and disbelief, Peter scrawled his name on the dotted line thrust at him. He picked up the tiny slip he received in return and looked for his quarry.

There she was, working at a laptop in one of the corners. He strolled over in the nonchalant way he had been instructed to.

''Morning,' he said. 'Mind if I join you?'

'Feel free,' said the woman, 'rather busy, though.'

'Haven't we met before?' said Peter, rather pleased with how well he was handling things.

'Don't think so,' said the woman. 'How's the market?'

'Up thirty,' said Peter and sipped at the wine, which seemed even worse than the previous week's. He resolved to try a different one next time.

'Really,' said the woman. 'What volume?'

'Low,' said Peter, 'but I think we're getting triangular consolidation.'

'Overbought, in my opinion,' said the woman. 'But telecoms are attractive if volume picks up.'

'Funny you should say that,' said Peter excitedly, 'that is the one sector where volume is quite strong.'

Peter suddenly started enjoying himself. A man at the next table soon chipped in to their conversation and they were joined by another. Before long there was a full circle and Peter was at the centre. This was fun! Even the wine didn't taste too bad. Telecoms were the star. Buy telecoms, for sure. One of the men at the edge of the circle left in a hurry, quickly followed by another. Suddenly there was a flood and Peter was left alone with the woman.

'Nice one,' she said. 'But you know what it's like nowadays… hope we don't get done for false rumours… About another matter. Slip it under my bum, will you?'

'Eh?' said Peter, suddenly coming down to earth. 'Oh, yes.' He pushed the envelope where he had been told.

'Don't make it so obvious,' said the woman. 'Couldn't you… give the impression you're giving me a gentle caress around there?'

'Eh?' gasped Peter.

'Now you leave and I'll see you next week.'

'What's your name?' said Peter.

'Never mind' came the response. 'Next week look out for a redhead. OK?'

'But I thought you said you'd see me next week?'

'Of course I will,' she responded. 'Now get going so I can get off too'.

Mystified, Peter went back up into the real world. Funny sort of bar that was. Nice girl. Clever. Good looks. A bit old for him, perhaps?

Peter began to enjoy his weekly visits to The Bar. He abandoned Pouilly fumé and found a schooner of dry sherry very much more to his taste. No one at the office seemed to mention the price of these drinks, even though a glass cost almost as much as he had to pay for a whole bottle in the supermarket. He enjoyed meeting his friend, whose style of clothes and hair changed dramatically every week. It was not always easy to recognize her, since she often wore a wig. They only ever chatted about the market, although she once asked him where he lived. After one particularly lively session on market theory he asked whether she would like another drink, but a glance at her watch gave him the answer. 'You know,' she said, 'if you made an effort, you could look quite presentable. I'll bring you a card next time.' She did: it was for a gentlemen's outfitter. 'Happened to be passing them on the way here,' she said. 'Tell them to smarten you up.' 'Nice!' she said appreciatively the following week. 'Try this next.' It was an optician. A dentist followed. All costly stuff, but Peter felt transformed. His friend smiled encouragingly at every stage. He got much better at sliding envelopes under her bottom, and once felt strongly inclined to give her a pinch. 'You look very... glamorous today,' he managed. 'But... why do you look so different every week?'

She looked at him with a smile and then broke into a laugh.

'Well,' she said, 'wouldn't do to be seen with the same man too often, would it!'

'I suppose not', said Peter. 'I know I shouldn't ask, but... what's in those envelopes I give you?'

'Hmm,' she said. 'God only knows, but you've probably got some idea'

'No,' said Peter.

'Really?' she said. 'M-L really is a sharp card. Get me drunk some day and I'll tell you what I think's in them.... But it's getting on for twelve, slip the envelope in the usual place, I need to be off.'

Peter messed up the key bit and started to apologise.

'You really are cute,' said the woman. 'But I gotta go.'

'Oh,' said Peter. 'See you next week'.

Peter liked working late at the office. Things relaxed the moment 4.30 arrived and the dealing stopped, and then there was another half hour or so as people tidied up their desks, did what they had promised to do at lunchtime, and loudly exchanged risqué jokes. Then there was a steady drift away to bars, tubes, railways, even to gymnasiums. The jokes got weaker, the secretaries had suddenly all disappeared, M-L was downing a whisky in some bar or other, and it was down to a hard core of bachelors more keen on making money than chatting up girls, henpecked husbands reluctant to return to henpecking, cleaners picking up newspapers and all sorts of other paper from the floor... and Peter, who would set about analysing the day's business, keep a very firm eye on New York (but he was never allowed to trade in those stocks, 'corrupt market' M-L had declared, and that was that), and then, after a couple of hours, drop out for a quick bite to eat.

But he would soon be back, chatting with the few faithfuls who were eager to test out on him their views for the following morning, looking at the hourly charts of some of his new smaller company hopefuls, reflecting on where he might have done better, and... learning Japanese. There was one insomniac in the office, Charlie, who always traded for the first hour of the Tokyo market and sometimes, it was reputed, fell asleep at his desk just as the early birders were drifting in. It was Charlie who had introduced Peter to the Far East, who had been impressed with how quickly he had picked up the different style there, and who had challenged him to learn a few words of the strange language. Compared with Ancient Greek, Japanese was not too bad. A lot of hard learning, true, but logical, grammatical, fascinating. He now had three evening lessons a week from a Japanese speaker, and he was soon able to see his way round the relevant economic jargon and pass on bits of breaking news. And, before long, he learnt to see the impact it would have on local share prices. Typhoons, of course, were bad for insurers, great for builders, difficulties with China were worse than difficulties with the States, Japanese housewives controlled the retail market, and their psychology was different from British housewives, that was for sure...

One night he and Charlie felt they were on to something. A news bulletin hit the screen about an earthquake in the southern part of the country. 'Good for builders,' said Peter; 'yep, and bad for insurers,' said Charlie. 'Get the details direct from US monitors, I would say. The Japs will keep really bad news quiet a bit longer than they should. I'll sell the big insurers, just in case... if it's the south, which are the big builders there?' Just then M-L strode in.

'Ah,' he bellowed, 'great to see someone at work, just as long as it's not analysing that awful corrupt place across the pond, why only the other day I came across a most appalling case of insider dealing there, book-cooking, fraud at the highest level, all to fund lifestyles we couldn't dream of... what are you looking at?'

'Japan,' said Peter, 'bad news in the south, Charlie is about to start trading insurers for builders, I'm just trying to get the full details from the US. Oh dear,' he said, 'it looks really bad. Seven on the Richter, they reckon, epicentre just off the coast of Kobe. Bad for ships as well, then.'

'Open me a monitor!' demanded M-L. 'What's your limit, Charlie? Forget that, use this code. Do you remember when this happened last? I do. Trade to the limit and double quick. It's sad there's so much to be made out of disaster, but it's like when you're on the racing track, if you see someone's had a spill, increase your speed while all the others ease off in fear or deference. Thistle, what are you like on the Jap shipbrokers?'

Peter reeled off three names. He felt in his element. 'likely to be an impact on our own, of course,' he continued, 'the obvious two, and especially the three in the US.'

'Keep the US out of this!' snarled M-L. 'Name me their insurers. Charlie, how do we short them? Thistle, what are their builders? Any specialists in ports? There'll be repercussions elsewhere. Where?' he asked Peter. He had his answer immediately. 'Good,' he said. 'Well, then there'll be the Aid brigade, where do they work from out there?'

For the next fifteen minutes Peter was shouting out names, looking at bulletins for information, calling out share movements; Charlie and he each had three screens going, M-L was rasping orders, they occasionally lost track of their dealing but they kept going in the conviction they were right. They had been so far. Most of their ideas were galloping. After only twenty minutes M-L called a halt. 'Thistle, what's the latest bulletin say? I see. Sounds like it could be not quite so bad. OK, be brutal. Take profits on everything. Yes, everything,' he said. 'Shorts and all.' It took almost half an hour to get everything straight, but as they were finishing, prices in Japan were clearly turning.

'Gods, what timing!' said M-L. 'How much d'you reckon we made there, Charlie? Yes, of course very approximately. As much as ten percent! Really? Damn good, though I say it myself. There's a massive bonus coming to you for spotting this. Really? Couldn't have done it without Thistle? Hoho, he's a cool laddie. One of the best decisions in my life employing him! And what he doesn't know about women's underwear...'

He beamed at Peter. 'Thistle! Same bonus as Charlie! Six figures, I suspect.'

'Wow, sir,' said Peter. 'Thank you, sir.'

M-L strode off confidently. He paused only to light his pipe and break wind loudly as he made his way to his office. 'Aaaah, that's better,' he said. Peter wasn't quite sure what he was referring to. M-L left open his door and the sound of a cork was soon to be heard.

'Thistlethwaite!' he boomed. Peter hurried along. M-L had his feet up on his desk, revealing a very worn pair of soles and a very large hole in his socks. Him a millionaire? But the whisky bottle did look particularly glamorous...

'Aaaah,' belched M-L as he picked up a delicate tumbler. 'Get me a drop of water, will you?'

Peter returned with the requested beverage. M-L's glass

was already empty. He half filled it again and filled the rest with the water. 'Thistle,' he said. 'Never enjoyed myself so much in years! Just like the old times! When you need a favour from me, you call it in, right!'

'Yes, sir,' said Peter. 'Thank you, sir.'

Peter's bonus came through the next week, and the following one he had moved into a luxury penthouse suite with a view of the Thames. Ah, he thought, this *would* impress Jane!

One late Spring day Peter received a letter from St Badley's. It was indeed from Jane. She'd got his address from Paul Challoner, who had told the whole College how well he was doing. Paul hadn't got the job. Jane was coming to an office near Bishopsgate for an interview with 'the Revenue' and wondered whether they could meet for a 'quick half'?

Peter replied cautiously, suggesting they meet for a drink in his favourite wine bar. Jane responded that she wasn't sure about drinks in such expensive places, but she knew things were different in the City, so as long as it was quiet, she'd be very pleased.

Peter wasn't quite sure what to make of Jane now. He had to admit that he had really quite fancied her at College, but mixing with so many new people had given him much higher hopes, even if he hadn't yet dare chat anyone up properly; and he seemed to have lost his Crucifix dream, who blushed madly every time she saw him and moved to the other side of the room. So he had to admit that showing off his new social skills in The Bar was very, very tempting. Jane's interview was on Friday morning, so he suggested they meet at 12, which would ensure his morning assignment was well complete. He began to think more about Jane. A scholar! Legs a bit thin, but maybe she would be wearing a suit?

The day arrived and Peter bounced down the steps to the Bar even more briskly than usual. He would be chatting up *two* women in one morning! This was the life!

'What's your name,' he said to his Friday friend, after they had had their usual chat.

'Best not to know,' replied Friday, 'and don't come up to me in quite such a friendly way. Do it like you used to, as if you were trying to chat me up, or someone'll get wise.'

She was blonde today, with long flowing hair, and she was wearing a short skirt. Her legs looked lovely. Pity Jane couldn't see him now.

'Anyway, you're mind's on other things,' she noted. 'It's my legs, isn't it?'

'No!' said Peter, blushing. 'Well... a bit. Sorry. A lot. But I'm seeing someone from Oxford I used to know and I'm not sure now whether I want to have a drink with her. She's not a bit like you. You're so... frank. She's a bit... more...'

'Reticent? Frigid?'

'Er... yes, I mean, maybe, I mean.... but...but she's very clever. A scholar!'

'Oh,' said the girl. 'What makes you think I wasn't a scholar when I was up at Oxford?'

'Really?' said Peter. 'Gosh!'

'Gotta go,' said the girl. 'Where's your envelope?'

Peter managed the discreet action rather well this time and clearly enjoyed it.

'You're sometimes quite good at that,' she said. 'Hmmm. I wonder. See you next week. What would you like me to dress in then, you naughty boy?' And with that she winked at him and was off.

'*Naughty boy*?' Ooh-la-la, that brought back memories! Peter was so lost in delightful thoughts that he barely noticed Jane come into the bar. She was indeed wearing a suit.

'I thought you'd be waiting for me upstairs,' she complained.

'Oh, sorry,' said Peter. 'Er... business with a colleague. Can I get you a drink? Sherry?'

'A small one,' said Jane, seeing the size of Peter's glass.

'How did you get on at the interview,' asked Peter.

'I don't know,' said Jane. 'They seemed awfully uninterested and then they asked me whether I knew anyone in the City. I said I knew you and that you worked for Mason-Legge. They really seemed to wake up then. I told them we were having a drink together, and they seemed delighted. I think they were impressed in my social skills... and my networking,' she added with a smile. 'Oh, this sherry's quite nice.'

Three days later Peter got a letter. Jane had got the job. They would be working quite close by. Well, that had to be good news. Surely?

Chapter Seven

'Oh, by the way, Thistle,' said M-L one morning. 'We're interviewing a few hopefuls later on this afternoon. Firm's expanding even further. Need more top quality people like you. Girl from St B's on the list. You like to be on the interview panel? That mad psychologist drops in to give them the once-over first, unsettle them, you know the drill, then they're over to us.'

'Gosh, yes, sir,' said Peter. 'That will be exciting. A girl from St B's! An economist, perhaps?'

'Hope not', said M-L. 'Bloody waste of time all this economics garbage. Gets in the way of instinct and common sense. Psychology's a much better subject. What were you studying, by the way... can't remember what I did. English? No, History. No...Yes, English, yes, yes, that's how I got my first article published in the *Racing Post* – the Fellow in English recommended me. What a character! Dreadful judge of horses, though. And as for the real fillies... I think he's on his fourth. Poor sod.'

Peter looked a bit disapproving at the use of such language, and M-L noticed.

'There's only one thing wrong with you, Thistle', he declared, but in a slightly benevolent tone. 'You're bloody awful at bad language! You've got to learn to b and eff if you want to become a successful City man!'

'I wish I could,' said Peter, 'but it's not easy. My father is a vicar, you know...'

'Eff all vicars!' trumpeted M-L. 'A good blast of the eff machine against life, love and the church never did anyone any harm!'

'I bow to your superior experience,' said Peter, delighted he could adapt what he had once heard the Dean of St B's use, rather facetiously, 'but actually... euphemism can be much more effective that the real thing.'

'Eh?' said M-L. 'Euphemism? Give me an example!'

'Well,' said Peter, 'let's see… If you take a well-known phrase like 'French without tears' and then adapt it, I wouldn't say what *you'd* say…'

'Fucking without tears! Nice one!' said M-L, then, a little embarrassed, 'well, what would *you* say, then?'

'Well, maybe "kissing without tears", but as long as the person you're talking to knows what you really mean, then the joke is a double one.'

'So,' went on Peter, 'since you now know exactly what the sub-text actually is, I could go on and you would get an intellectual thrill!'

'Sub-text! Intellectual thrill! Is that what you learn at St B's nowadays? Bloody hell! But go on…'

'OK,' said Peter, 'but you must join in! I'll start. The idea is to get a well-known phrase, right?'

'Get on with it, man!'

'Kissing… may seriously damage your health.'

'Hohoho!' said M-L, 'hmm… That's good. Er…It's kissing that makes the world go round?'

'You've got it!' said Peter. 'Now then, see how long you can keep it up! Kissing for fun!'

'Kissing for profit!'

'Do you *sincerely* want to be kissed?'

'Hmm… How to kiss on five dollars a day!'

'Kissing on a diet.'

'Teaching kissing.'

'I'm kissed, you're kissed.'

'Kissing in bed.'

'Kisses I have known.'

'Kiss me quick!'

'Kissing awful.'

'Kissers of the world, unite!'

'Who kisses who?'

'Quick kisses.'

'Slow kisses'

'Medium kisses.'

'Kissers I have known.'

'Kissing in the upper classes.'

'Kissing the upper classes.'

'The right to kiss!'

'Kissing for the Olympics.'

'Kissing problems.'

'Kissing answers.'

'In the beginning was the...'

'Stop!' said Peter. 'if there's one thing I struggle with it's blasphemy!'

'But come on now,' said M-L smugly. 'In the beginning was the kiss, there must have been, mustn't there... Do you know what, Thistle? You've taught me something.'

The afternoon 'interview panel' comprised just the two of them. Peter had worked out a few questions, but he only got to ask them if M-L hadn't dispatched the candidate after five minutes. M-L summed them up fairly briskly:

'Nice, but dim.'

'Posh but thick.'

'Hopeful, but not very hungry.'

'All frills and no knickers.'

'No staying power.'

At last M-L grew tired and let Peter have a crack.

'Why do you want to be a stockbroker?'

'Because I want to earn huge sums of money.'

'Why should you sometimes try to catch a falling knife?'

'Because you only need to catch one in five to make a killing.'

'What has the study of Economics got to do with the stock market?'

'It provides brokers with some useful vocabulary and pseudo-science to justify their actions.'

'Nice questions you put there,' said M-L. 'Damn good. We'll take him and you'll train him for the first two weeks. He's too cocky, but he's hungry. Now then, girl from St B's next... let's see... Frances Howard? Remember her?'

'I vaguely remember the name,' said Peter, 'I think… Oh God!…Oh no!... It couldn't possibly be…'

Frankie strode confidently in. She looked fantastic.

'Sit down, please,' cooed M-L, lowering his head to see if he could glimpse any flesh above the sheer black stockings. Frankie had crossed her legs exquisitely. Peter wasn't sure whether it was from excitement or something else, but M-L knocked some papers on the floor and had to get down on his knees to pick them up. While he was doing so Frankie slowly re-crossed her knees. M-L gave a gasp and got back into his chair.

'Now then,' he said, 'have you ever been in a stockbroker's den before?'

'My father used to work for OB Securities, I visited the firm several times and Mr Bumser once suggested I was the type who would get on quite well here.'

'Indeed,' said M-L. 'But why didn't you apply to Bumser's?'

'Very good firm, but too much on the gilts side for my liking, I'd prefer to be in a totally equity-based firm.'

'But Bumser's have made a lot of money out of trading gilts,' said M-L deferentially.

'Yes,' said Frankie, 'that's true, but that's all very routine stuff, not much imagination, not much flair, I'd like to be dealing by the second, hedging, happily losing a few thousand here if I can get a ten thousand there, constantly searching for the winners and then letting them run.'

Frankie had uncrossed her knees and was leaning forward in earnest. The neckline on her blouse was poised between modesty and the suggestion of something else. Peter could just about fancy he could catch a glimpse of a blue lacey bra without being able to swear to it. Being well endowed helped, or didn't, depending on your perspective.

'I like you,' said M-L. 'But you must let my principal assistant put a few questions,' and he turned beamingly to Peter.

'Ms Howard, are you a teamworker?'

'I love being in teams, I am totally committed to the concept and would do anything to maintain the life and integrity of any team to which I belonged.'

'Excellent,' said Peter. He could hear M-L was purring.

'You were at St Badley's, I believe, were you in any teams there?'

'Oh yes,' said Frankie, 'I was in the netball team and I rowed in the First Women's Boat. I was secretary of the Boat Club for one term too. And I often acted.' She sat back slightly as she said this, pulling back her shoulders and allowing her exceptional breasts their best advantage.

'Did you?' said Peter. 'Absolutely splendid.' M-L was rubbing his hands.

'Any intellectual societies… like the Philosophy or the Chess Club?' M-L was totally unbothered by the curt 'no'.

'Social groups…? Er…' Peter took off his trendy glasses, shut his mouth so that his perfect teeth remained hidden, and adopted a very studious look… 'like… *The Virgins*?'

'*The Virgins*?' exclaimed M-L. 'What on earth…? There were plenty of them around in my time, but all, alas, of the male variety! But nowadays? Ye gods! You're joking! Who are they?'

Frankie had gone distinctly pale. Her sexual poise had vanished. She was staring at Peter in disbelief.

'Ah,' said Peter to M-L, 'don't be deceived by the name! *The Virgins* were a select group of young women who knew how to dress well, drink well, and have a really good time. Why, undoubtedly the best occasion in my entire life was when I attended one of their meetings.'

Frankie looked as if she was going to bolt for the door.

'Any member of that society,' went on Peter, 'would be an excellent acquisition for this firm.'

'Damn right!' said M-L. 'Not enough women get to have a really good time nowadays. Good on you, girl! The job's yours. Hang around for ten minutes or so, we'll get though the next hopeless hopefuls, and have a drink together.'

'Damn good interviewing technique!' he muttered to Peter. 'Good old St B's!'

Frankie had recovered her cool a little by the time M-L had over-eagerly despatched the three final candidates.

'Well done,' he said to her, shaking her hand and planting an enormous kiss on each of her glowing cheeks. 'We selected two out of ten today, and must have rejected a hundred before interview. We pride ourselves on our selection methods here. Oh, by the way, how did you get on with the trick cyclist? Never mind, he often gets things wrong. Here, have a drink and young Thistle will give you a tour of the place. When can you start?'

Peter enjoyed taking Frankie round the main rooms, explaining who did what, where the back office was, who were the reliable sources of information, but he could see she was desperately uncomfortable. So was he. When they were near the end he decided to take a risk.

'Sorry about my last question,' he said, 'but it didn't do you any harm, did it?'

'It *was* you, wasn't it?' said Frankie. 'There have only been two occasions in my life when I have been really embarrassed – the first when I had to do it with you, and the second half an hour ago. I am most terribly sorry about the first. Do you know why I had to?'

'Why you *had* to?' gasped Peter.

'Can we go for a drink somewhere, and I'll tell you all about it? We were all mortified when you were sent down. So quickly. No one had a chance to protest. If I can ever make it up to you in any way…'

'The market closes in ten minutes,' said Peter. Let me close some positions and then let me take you to a bar I know. I'm intrigued at why you *had* to.'

Peter proudly took Frankie down to the Bar. The barmaid smiled at his conquest with approval. She usually gave him a wink on Fridays, but on this occasion she gave him something closer to a broad grin. And the wink that followed was a bit too meaningful for comfort. But it made Peter feel very good.

'What would you like?' he asked Frankie. 'I often have Pouilly fumé.'

'Wow,' said Frankie, 'all right by me.'

Peter signed the chit with a flourish, suddenly realising that entertaining new employees might not count, but he also realised that he was beyond caring. What had Frankie said… Why she *had* to?

'It was actually all about teams,' said Frankie… and little by little she put Peter in the picture. The tussle between Big Jo and Blondilocks, Frankie's acceptance of her punishment, her amazement that Peter's crown jewels were actually some of the finest she'd seen, the conviction he'd been a virgin, Big Jo's saving the day, their relief and then their terrible sense of guilt at Peter's fate, their determination to get rid of the Bursar and the Dean, and then the news Peter had somehow landed a great job in the City.

'I am so sorry,' she said. 'But it doesn't seem to have done you much harm, actually. You're transformed! And you're obviously nowhere near a virgin now!'

'Well, believe it or not,' said Peter, 'those few minutes with you were the best, and only, ones of my sexual life. I may have been successful in the City, but not with women. I think deep down I am a bit scared of you all. My father, you see, is a vicar.'

'You poor thing,' said Frankie. 'Mine's a Bishop. They're a lot more laid back. Hey, I wonder… Look… maybe this is how I can make things up to you. Where do you live?'

Ten minutes later they were in the penthouse.

Chapter Eight

'Nice place,' said Frankie.

'Yes,' said Peter. 'It costs a fortune, but there are great views. Especially at night. Hey, come over here and look out of the big window.'

Frankie looked in admiration as Peter pointed out the sights.

'Oh,' he said suddenly, 'can I get you a drink? A glass of... sherry, perhaps?'

'Look,' said Frankie, 'I have come here to help you, and by god, you don't half need a few tips. Don't you?'

'Yes, please,' said Peter.

'OK, I'm going to have to give you a crash course. It won't be like this with everyone, but I'll give you a speeded up version of how it might go...

'Let's start again. We both know why I might have come here, right? So when I enter you should offer to take my jacket. I don't need to take it off, I'm not particularly hot, but if I do, that's a sign I'm interested. OK?'

'Oh,' said Peter.

'Then you offer me a drink, all casual like, you mention a glass of water first – I hope you've got really fancy fizzy stuff – most people don't want to get too drunk if they're in the mood for real seduction, and they don't like strong liquor flung in their face as the only alternative, so maybe a glass of white wine, maybe a spritzer...but actually... a small gin and tonic is best,' she added. 'You can use a lot of tonic if you like. And really good gin helps.

'Then you take me over to the window and gently, casually, put your arm around my shoulder – don't *grab* me as most blokes usually do – as you turn me round from one side of the view to the other. If I push your arm off, that means get lost – at least for the time being. If I don't, that's another signal. Gottit?'

'Wow,' said Peter, 'I'm learning! But are you sure all women are like this?'

'Of course!' said Frankie. 'Just keep going until I gently push you away, or I'm obviously upset, or I simply say "no".'

'Now,' she said, 'take in how I'm standing in relation to you. Have you read any books on body language? That might be a good start. Look, if I'm facing you straight on, and looking into your eyes and smiling, that means I'm very interested in you. And, if you look straight at me, you might find something complimentary to say.'

'Er…' said Peter, feeling a bit uneasy.

'Nice earrings?' suggested Frankie in desperation.

'Very nice,' said Peter, 'but actually, maybe I shouldn't say this… but your eyes are wonderful… they remind me of a line in Ovid.'

'For God's sake,' said Frankie. 'What do you mean, you "shouldn't say this"! Course you damn well should, and then you ruin it with a reference to bloody Ovid!'

'Sorry,' said Peter, 'but they really do! They are smouldering like a fire about to burst into flame, but at the same time they are so soft and yet so powerful, so…'

'Hmmm,' said Frankie. 'A bit cheesy, but… I like it. Anything else?'

'Well, maybe I… the colour of your cheeks is like… yes, it really is like a rose, it's wonderful, and together with your smouldering eyes, it makes me want to plant a gentle kiss on each of your beautiful eyelids, and oh god, I'm getting terribly excited.'

'Not bad, not bad at all,' said Frankie encouragingly and with a warm smile. 'And saying you are terribly excited is quite a good line. I've never had that before. Anything else?' she asked, throwing back her shoulders and running her fingers down his chest.

'Oh God,' said Peter, 'you've got the most marvellous figure, and those black stockings are such a turn-on too, I… I… want to give you a kiss… on each of your…'

'Go ahead', said Frankie, pushing her breasts forward slightly. 'What sort of a bra do you think I've got on?'

Realising Peter needed a bit of help, she suggested:

'Why don't you say something like "I bet you've got a fantastic bra", and then *gently* undo my top buttons to have a look at it. And if I say nothing, you unbutton the rest.'

Peter fumbled with the top buttons, exposing the top of the lacey blue bra which revealed almost as much of Frankie's breasts as it covered.

He gulped and somehow managed to undo the other buttons.

'Now,' said Frankie, 'gently slip it off!'

'Gods,' said Peter, 'I've never been so excited since we did it last time!'

'Good,' said Frankie, 'now take it easy for a bit, perhaps pull me towards you and give me a gentle hug, *gentle*, right? Good, that's nice, now, how about my hair – I forgot, you should have got my hairband out a while ago, hey, that's right, clever you. Hmm. Now we really would need to be like this for a little while, but I suddenly realise I've got no idea what time it is and I've got to go somewhere else later, so look, why don't pay attention to my skirt? What do you reckon to my belt?'

'I don't know why,' said Peter, but I find it very sexy.'

'So you should at the price it cost,' laughed Frankie, 'but why don't you slip it off?'

To his amazement Peter managed the unbuckling first time, and gently withdrew the belt through its loops.

'Now,' said Frankie, 'does that belt give you any ideas?'

Peter's heart was in his mouth again. What on earth could he do? But it was brainwave time. He pulled the belt across Frankie's bottom and pulled her gently towards him.

'Not bad!' said Frankie. 'Not what I had in mind, but very good. Now, why don't you slowly find the zip on my skirt – no, other side – good, pull it down, right, now undo the hook… use both hands if you must – right, now let my skirt go…'

Peter heard something slip silkily to the floor. He stepped back

'Oh my god!' he said. 'You… you… are… incredible… you…'

Frankie smiled appreciatively. 'I believe you,' she smiled. 'Now, would you like to kiss my neck…'

Just then there was the ring of a mobile.

'Shit,' said Frankie. She moved over to her handbag. 'Shit' she said again, 'what's the time? Hello, Dick. Yes, sorry. Yes, I know I said I'd phone straight after but there wasn't a chance – I got the job. Yes! Really! So as you can imagine, there's been a pretty steep learning curve for me. Where are you? Sorry. Yes, I'll be there in twenty minutes. Have another drink on me!'

Frankie looked very embarrassed. 'Well,' she said, 'you probably worked that out. My boyfriend. You may not believe this, but I was enjoying being with you. Very much, actually. But I'll have to sprint. There'll be another time, I'm sure.'

'Yes,' said Peter, 'I'm sure. That was… wonderful.'

Frankie had her clothes on within seconds, threw some perfume over her neck, gave Peter a firm kiss on the lips, and was gone.

'Shit,' said Peter. 'Damn, blast and bloody hell.'

He decided to go for a walk. He wanted a bit of company, but there was no point in going back to the office. He padded along Bishopsgate, with an unsettling mixture of elation and total frustration. He felt thirsty, so he turned towards one of the few haunts he knew. He descended the steps to find the place deserted. All the regulars were probably back at their screens or back at home.

'Hello, darling,' said the barmaid, obviously delighted to have a customer. 'Late for you! I liked your new friend! Impressive! That was quick work, though. It's only gone half past seven. I didn't have the impression you were such a fast worker!'

'I'm not,' said Peter, 'I'm a total and utter failure'.

'Oh dear,' said the barmaid, 'did she dump you? You didn't push it too fast, did you?'

'I didn't push it at all,' said Peter forlornly.

'Here,' said the barmaid, 'get this down you. You're in bad shape. Have it on the house. Nothing like a G and T to pick you up. Tell me what went wrong.'

Peter looked round. The bar was indeed empty. He took a gulp of his drink. 'Ah, that's better,' he said. 'Hey, would you like one?'

'That's nice of you, pet. That's very nice indeed. Not many people offer me drinks nowadays. Don't mind if I do. I close at nine and I doubt whether I'll get another customer. I was just going to do my books. Aaah, that's better. Here, you have another one too. Cheer up!' She gave his hand a gentle squeeze.

'Now then, tell me all about it. We can settle up later.'

'Oh, god,' said Peter. 'I suppose I better come clean. It began in Oxford, when I was blindfolded and forced to have sex with a woman.'

'Blimey!' said the barmaid. 'I knew they got up to some strange things in Oxford, but that takes the biscuit. Was it horrible?'

'No, it was fantastic. It was my first time, you see. And then, blow me,' he took another gulp of his G & T, 'aaah, that's better... that woman I was in with before, she was the one that did it.'

'What!!' said the barmaid.

'To make up for it she said she'd show me how to seduce someone properly, and it was going brilliantly until her mobile went and she had to trot off to her boyfriend.'

'You poor thing,' said the barmaid, in a voice as if she meant it. 'How far did you get?'

'Well, she'd just taught me how to unzip a skirt.'

'Hmmm,' said the barmaid, a mixture of disbelief and admiration. 'Would you like to go a little further some time?' And she winked.

Peter looked at her. She must be twice his age, but she had a wicked smile.

'What a lovely smile you've got,' he said.

'Hey, what do you need to know about seduction?'

came the reply. 'Look, where is your place? Nearby I suppose? I'll come round as soon as I've done. Won't be much after nine. What's the address? Do you really want me to finish off your education? I can take you a little bit further than slipping off a skirt…'

Peter's doorbell rang bang on nine. 'Come in,' he said. 'Hey, you look lovely! Can I take your jacket? Would you like something to drink? Perhaps some fizzy water after your hard day? Or a glass of white wine?' He realised he was pushing it, since he didn't yet have any fizzy water or white wine, so he quickly continued, 'or a glass of really good… sherry?'

'Hmm, that would be nice,' said the barmaid, 'but let me admire your pad first. My name's Eileen. What's yours?'

'Peter.'

'That's a nice name. Do you like "Eileen"?'

'Yes, it's lovely. Just like your… face.'

'Thank you,' she said, looking really pleased. She was facing him directly. Peter was getting a bit scared.

'Oh,' he said, 'come and see the view'. He led her over to the window and then had an inspiration. 'It's better in the dark,' he said, 'I'll just switch off the light.'

It was indeed quite romantic with the lights over the City. He came back to her, gently put his arm round her shoulder and pulled her to one side. 'Look, he said, 'you can just see the top of the Wheel over there, and look out the other window, there's the Gherkin!'

'It's great,' she said. 'Where's my sherry?'

'Ooops, sorry,' said Peter. 'It was just so good holding you like that I completely forgot.'

Eileen looked at him intently. 'Either you are a damn good liar, or you have learnt a hell of a lot in a short time, or…or… do you really like my name?'

'Of course!' said Peter softly. 'And what lovely earrings you have. And gosh, now I get really close to you, what lovely eyes. They really smoulder, they do, they remind me of...'

'Yes?'

'A line from a famous Roman poet. Oh, and your hair, it's a lovely colour.'

They were already very close to each other.

'Gosh,' said Peter, 'I suppose I shouldn't say this, but you do make me feel very excited. What a... what a...'

'Yes..?'

'I shouldn't say this either, but... you have a fantastic figure.' She came even closer. He put out his arms and pulled her to him.

'Hey,' she said, 'you *are* excited, you naughty boy!'

Naughty boy! Ooh...

Peter had forgotten the next line. He simply went straight to the top button of her blouse. And then the second.

'Hey, you're a bit keen! Anyone would think you're trying to get a view of my bra!'

'Ah yes,' said Peter, 'I bet it is a really sexy one'. The third button had now gone. 'Wow,' he said. 'it really *is* fantastic!'

Eileen smiled. Her buttons undid a lot easier than Frankie's and he soon had them all opened. Wow! Her breasts weren't as full as Frankie's and her bra didn't expose quite so much; but she was breathing quite deeply, and Peter eagerly followed each rise and fall of her chest. He pulled her to him again, now rather worried about the next bit.

'You are really cute,' said the barmaid. 'I like you. You really sound as if you mean it.'

'Of course I do', said Peter. 'It's thrilling holding you like this.' He took up courage and started searching for her zip.

'Hey,' she said, 'you make a woman feel so good that she's not too bothered when you push it!' And she helped him undo the hook, which was proving troublesome. The skirt slipped to the floor and Peter stepped back. Not quite the glamour of Frankie's suspender belt, and there was a big tear in her tights near the top.

'Wow!' he said. 'Wow. You look…'

'Yes?'

'Ravishingly sexy and desirable and boy, do I want you!'

'Hmmm,' said the barmaid, 'well, you're welcome. I might even want you…'

Peter's face then said it all.

'What's the matter? What have I done wrong?'

'I'm sorry, I just… don't know what to do next…'

'Oh you silly sausage! Well, first of all why not undo my bra? No, it undoes at the back. You could even… well, never mind. Why not pull down my tights? One side a little bit then the other side a little bit, yes, that's it.'

'You are wearing superb knickers,' said Peter, suppressing the contrast with Frankie's minimalist thongs.

'Thank you! Do you really think so? I'll put on some much better ones next time. Now why don't we slip off to your bed? The next bit might be easier lying down. No, don't turn on the light. And for heaven's sake take a few clothes off. Here, let me help…'

Peter awoke in the middle of the night to find he was being gently stroked between the legs.

'You awake? Yes? Now remember what I taught you? Ok, well let's do it again.'

For the first time in his life Peter was late in at the office.

M-L spotted him.

'Hohoho! I know why you're late!' he said. 'I saw you going off with that first-rate piece of crumpet! Tell me: have you been at it all night? You little rascal, you! I doubt whether there's anyone in this office who could teach you anything! What a bounder!'

What a start to the day, and, to cap it all, Jane had arrived in London and started work! She got in touch with him by email suggesting they meet. Dinner would be a very nice idea. Whoopee! After all he now knew…

Two days later he took Jane to a small Italian restaurant which was significantly busier at lunchtime than in the evening. They were rather close to the adjacent table, though, so the conversation was a bit restricted. Still, Peter had caught up fully with St B's. He was both nostalgic and, to his surprise, slightly bitter.

As they lingered over coffee, and the man on the next table started earnestly fondling his partner's knee, Peter found himself getting worked up and decided to put Plan A into action. He was quite pleased with it: 'Would you like to see my pad?' he would ask casually, 'it has some nice views, and,' to be added with a wink, 'there's a glass of something else if you'd like it.'

But Jane clearly had a Plan A too: 'Hmm….' she said in a low voice. 'This is a nice place, but not very private. And it would be good to talk about what you're doing these days. I don't like to ask in front of other people. And… I bet you've got a nice glass of sherry...?'

Peter couldn't believe his luck!

'Talk about what I'm doing?' he asked, not sure whether this was a modern euphemism. Maybe Jane was a bit more experienced than he thought!

'Oh, my life's pretty boring,' he said. 'Especially to scholars like you. But my pad does have some great views, it is *very* private, and I do indeed have a nice glass of something at the ready!' He paid the bill and they set on their way. As they left the restaurant Peter summoned up all his courage and took Jane's hand. She didn't stop him. What a start!

They had reached the penthouse. Peter tried to remember the key instruction: if she doesn't say no, keep going! But hang on, Jane seemed to be driving this! Where would it end up? In bed? Help! Still, he knew a thing or two now! Oh, yes!

Peter proudly opened the door and switched on the lights.

'Phew, nice place,' said Jane. 'They must pay you a lot at Mason-Legge.'

'Yes,' said Peter. 'The rent's a fortune, but it's got great views. Er… can I take your jacket?'

'Thank you,' said Jane.

'Crikey,' thought Peter. 'I'm in! But I better not switch off the lights. Yet…

'Let's look at the sights,' he said, 'but first, what about a drink? Some top class fizzy water after that wine we had in the restaurant? Or… a glass of white wine… a spritzer… maybe a G & T?'

'A gee and what?' said Jane.

'Sorry,' said Peter, 'City jargon! A gin and tonic. I have a top-rate gin, and you can add a fair bit of tonic if you like.'

'Alright, if you'll have one too,' said Jane. 'Mason-Legge must indeed pay you a lot. Do you get bonuses?'

'Oh, yes,' said Peter, going off to the kitchen and coming back with a two expensive-looking glasses, an elegant dark-green bottle, and two cans of tonic. Jane inspected the bottle approvingly.

'Hmmm,' she said, 'they must be big bonuses!'

'Not bad,' said Peter. 'Say when with the gin. It's quite strong,' he added after a few seconds, 'maybe you should top that up to the hilt with tonic?'

'Hmmm, very nice,' said Jane. 'Do you actually see a lot of the big man himself?'

'Oh yes, every day. He and I get on like a house on fire. Hey, come over here and look out of the big window.'

Peter casually put his arm round Jane's shoulder and turned her to the left, and then the right, pointing out the sights.

'Wow,' he thought, 'this is actually pretty easy!'

'And…er… do you do anything together at times?'

'Oh yes,' said Peter, recalling this was the moment to face Jane directly. 'Here's to M-L,' he said, raising his glass, 'the source of my earnings!'

Jane was looking intently at him. Great!

'That's very interesting,' she said, 'do you ever... trade together?'

'What lovely earrings!' said Peter.

'Er... thank you,' said Jane. 'What sort of things do you trade?'

'Well,' said Peter, 'we traded the Japanese market intensely one night, must have made the firm up to ten million.'

'How did you know what to trade?' asked Jane.

'Oh, I check the market almost every night watching out for anomalies, but that night there'd been an earthquake and you just had to be resolute.'

'Oh,' said Jane, and took another sip of her drink.

'Do you know,' said Peter, 'your eyes remind me from a line from Ovid! Do you know that one where the woman's eyes make him think of something smouldering like a fire about to burst into flame, but at the same time they are so soft and yet so powerful, so...'

'Do you do anything else with him... or for him?' asked Jane.

'I sometimes run the odd errand, deliver the odd letter...' It's now or never he thought, she hasn't said 'no' to anything.

'You are looking fantastic tonight. I bet you have the most amazing black bra on,' and he reached up to her top button.

Perhaps that was a bit of a risk and Jane seemed to flinch slightly, but maybe she was just getting a bit excited, because she went on, quite calmly, 'oh, what sort of letters?'

'I don't know,' said Peter, half-expecting a 'no', but already on the second button, 'they're private'.

'Does he send you regularly?'

'Oh, yes, every Friday'.

This was a dream! This was an absolute bloody dream! If only he'd known this when he had been at St B's! Hey, what if Frankie were to come back sometime? Hoho, she'd be so impressed by his subtlety! What a teacher she had been! He gently slid Jane's blouse over her shoulders. She was indeed wearing a black bra, but it was rather functional, and it wasn't very lacey. Still…

'Every Friday? Where do you take them?'

'The Downstairs Bar,' said Peter, gently pulling Jane towards him and confidently reaching for the hook in her waistband. No belt. Pity, he could have shown how subtle and experienced he was…

'Who do you give them to?'

'A woman. She's a redhead, but she often wears a wig, funny, isn't it!' The zip was already down and the skirt had slipped to the floor. This was effortless, absolutely effortless! Tights. Pity, but he mustn't compare everyone with Frankie. After all, Eileen had been pretty hot at the next bit, despite her pathetic tights! Jane's knickers were not very brief, alas, in fact… but never mind, they were a *scholar's* knickers! A *scholar's*! Just imagine that! If only he could tell them all about this back at the office! Peter gently put his thumbs into the tights and pulled them an inch or two down Jane's thighs.

'What time do you see her?'

He was going to have to get down on his knees to get these tights down her legs.

'Eleven forty-five on the dot.' He knelt down and suddenly found himself hit on the head with a tumbler.

'You dirty pig! What do you think you are doing? Get off me!'

'Eh?' said Peter rubbing his head. 'But I thought you… I thought… you wanted me to…'

'You dirty, molesting pervert! How dare you suggest I was encouraging you in any way whatsoever!'

She already had her skirt on and the top was on its way.

'But… but… I thought… I… you mean you didn't… then why did you let me…'

'Ugh!' said Jane, gathering up her jacket and making for the door. 'You are a vile monster. Don't see me out, you disgusting, despicable creature!'

The door banged. Peter sat down. But he'd done it just

like Frankie and Eileen had suggested. And she hadn't said a word until he'd touched her tights. What had he done wrong? Women!

Chapter Nine

Peter put the episode with Jane on a par with irregular cycles on the stock market. What signals had he missed? Had he been totally misled by those other helpful, willing females? If only he could talk it over with someone a bit more neutral, like his Friday friend…

Friday came quicker than usual, and Peter had made up his mind to broach the subject of Jane. Girl Friday was frank. She would know what he'd done wrong! He realised how much he liked her. And fancied her. What legs! He'd also decided on a new wine today. He'd tried various drinks over the past few weeks, and some of them had been quite exhilarating; but some had left him making very bad calls for the following two hours, and he'd decided those were something for after-work only. He'd heard an occasional order for 'Punt e mes', and he was now determined to try it. His plastic card seemed a passport to anything, and if life in the City wasn't about new experiences, what was? New experiences, boy, oh boy! What a week he'd had! With the usual envelope in his pocket, Peter eagerly descended the steps to the Bar. He grinned sheepishly at Eileen, and, with half an air of confidence, demanded 'I'd like Punt e mes, please!'

'Sure, darling,' came the reply, surprisingly loudly, 'punt e mes it is!' And then, under her breath, 'your usual girlfriend says go to the loo, get rid of that envelope in your pocket, and then join her.'

Peter was taken aback.

'Just do it,' said Eileen under her breath, and then, rather loudly, 'damn, need another bottle, won't be two ticks…'

Peter took the hint. Quite surprised about how casually he managed, it, he strolled off to the gents, took the envelope out of his pocket, tore it in half, and flushed it away. By the time he was back at the bar, a glass of dirty-looking red liquid was waiting for him.

He signed the chit. Eileen smiled.

'Drink it slowly,' she said, 'most people don't like caviar first time either... Er... when are you free again? Any chance of tonight?'

Peter coughed modestly and smiled. Ah, here was a woman who appreciated him! Could he tell Eileen the sorry tale of the night before? Maybe not.

'Not tonight, but tomorrow would be great,' he said, 'let's sort it out later.' He took a sip of his drink and winced. He wondered what caviar must be like and decided never to touch it. Puzzled by what was going on, he drifted over to where his girlfriend was sitting. He was most impressed how nonchalantly he was managing it all. If Jane could see him now! He sat down beside Friday, noticing for the first time how elegant her earrings were.

'Nice work,' she said. 'Now, pretend we're having a chat about the market. I'll slip something under your bum and then you'll give it back to me, right?'

Peter gave a puzzled 'OK' and took another sip of his wine. His grimace was softened by a soft caress of his buttock.

'Now,' said his girlfriend, 'pretend you're taking it out of your pocket, hold it up slightly but give the impression you're being a bit secretive, and slip it to me.'

Peter was very uneasy. The wine wasn't helping. He looked round the bar and saw two very un-City-like men in poorly-fitting suits and nondescript ties looking intently at him. They lowered their gaze when he caught their eye, and he used the moment to pluck something from the region of his pocket. As he gingerly held it aloft, the two men sprang up and approached him: 'would you like to give me that envelope, please?' said one, 'CID', said the other. I am Temporary Chief Detective Inspector Dick, and this is Acting Detective Inspector Shotwell.'

Peter grinned. 'You're joking,' he said.

'Alas, sir, we are far from joking,' said the TCDI, and he pulled out a badge. Peter looked at it, took it in his hand and seemed genuinely dumbfounded.

'Give me the envelope,' said the Chief Inspector, clearly annoyed that someone could not believe he was who he claimed to be.

Suddenly, Peter's girlfriend kicked into action.

'Inspector – I beg your pardon, Temporary Chief Inspector – my colleague and I were about to discuss the current situation in what is known as "Big Pharma" and we do not welcome this intrusion into our privacy. If you are intent on disrupting our deliberations, which may have important significance for press comment this evening, then will you kindly arrest us or go on your way. Shall I phone my lawyer?'

Dick took one look at Friday's face and winced. 'Inspector Shotwell,' he said, 'arrest this man on suspicion of passing market sensitive information. You, madam, may leave, but we shall without the shadow of a doubt be in touch with you before long. Tell me your name.'

'If you have any grounds for suspicion whatsoever,' said Friday, 'then you know my name, my place of residence, and the company for which I work. And if you do not, then the whole basis of this ridiculous arrest is fundamentally flawed.'

She rose and marched off. The policemen looked at her with a mixture of annoyance and disbelief. Peter smiled proudly.

Dick regained his composure. 'Cheeky madam,' he declared. 'We shall catch up with her this afternoon! Oh yes! Now then,' he said to Peter, 'come along with us!' He had regained his cool and was now glowing with satisfaction. 'But first put that envelope in here' – he brandished a plastic bag – 'and I will seal it in your presence.' He did so, quite expertly. Peter was impressed.

There was a police car at the top of the steps, and within minutes they were at a busy Police Station. Peter was bundled inside.

The Custody Sergeant looked at him with curiosity. 'What's the charge?' he asked.

'Passing market sensitive information' said Shotwell, 'in other words, insider dealing! We've got you, mate, and the rest of your gang. Someone'll get two years for this! Got to stamp it out once and for all! You silly prat! Think we haven't got a few inside informers ourselves?'

'That's enough!' said Dick. 'Take him to the cells! We'll be interviewing you in about quarter of an hour,' he said to Peter. 'And I advise you to come clean quick. Oh, do you want a solicitor?'

'Er... do you advise that I have a solicitor?' asked Peter.

'We can't advise you on that,' said Shotwell. 'But you can have one if you want. You can have it at public expense,' he said in a pained voice.

'No thank you,' said Peter. 'I am completely and utterly innocent'.

Dick and Shotwell smiled smugly.

The cell was dark and dismal, but at least it was quiet. Peter tried to work out what on earth he was going to say. Who was Friday anyway? Could he claim she really was just someone he chatted to about the market? Did he actually need a solicitor? What on earth was in that envelope? He groaned. But then he suddenly realised the game he'd been playing. How could he have been so stupid! Friday had obviously slipped him an empty envelope. She'd spotted the men in the bar and told Eileen what to say, pushing a fat tip over the counter, perhaps... But what could have been in the first envelope... Why had he been so naïve as never to ask? If it was inside information, why didn't M-L just phone it through to his pals? Maybe... it was just... love letters...?

The cell door opened with a bang. It was just like in the movies. 'Ah,' said Shotwell, 'come along with me.' Peter obligingly followed. They entered a small room with a tape recorder, where Dick was sitting and smiling. 'Now then', he said, 'Inspector Shotwell will conduct this interview and the first thing he will do is explain your rights…'

'Well, Mr Thistelthewaite,' said Shotwell, and then in a confidential tone of voice, 'can I call you "Peter", yes?'

'You can call me what you like.'

'Well, Peter, can you confirm you were in the Downstairs Bar in Bishopsgate between the hours of 11.15 and 11.25 this morning?'

'Yes of course I was,' said Peter. 'So were you.'

'Now, now,' said Shotwell. 'Don't be aggressive, just when we are getting somewhere.'

'And, Peter,' said Shotwell, reassuming a gentler voice, 'can you confirm you handed this envelope to Ms Miranda Shaftes-Mason?'

Peter looked at the envelope in the sealed bag.

'Yes,' he said, making a mental note of the name.

'Ah, said,' Shotwell, 'now we are *really* getting somewhere!'

'And,' he triumphed, 'can you tell me the name of the man who gave you that envelope, in other words, the name of your employer, Mr, I mean,' he spat it out, '*Sir* Richard Mason Legge? It was him, wasn't it!'

Peter was silent.

'So,' said Shotwell, 'you agree. You were in the Downstairs Bar between 11.15 and 11.25 this morning, you handed a letter to Ms Miranda Shaftes-Mason, and that letter was from your employer, Sir Richard Mason-Legge. And now,' he said, in a suddenly sweet tone, 'will you tell me the contents of that envelope?'

'No', said Peter.

'What do you mean, "no",' snarled Shotwell. 'Are you telling me you don't know – *or you won't tell me*?' He had an enormous grin of satisfaction.

'I don't know,' said Peter. 'I never tell a lie.'

Shotwell and Dick broke into laughter. 'And you in the City!' they shrieked. 'My word is my bond, eh!' Dick nodded towards the tape recorder and they both reverted to their dignified air.

'Very well,' said Shotwell. 'Would you like to open the sealed bag, open the envelope, and read us the contents.'

'No, I wouldn't like to,' said Peter. 'It's private.'

'Read it!' bellowed Shotwell.

Peter slowly broke the seal of the bag, gently ripped open the envelope, and pulled from inside a small piece of paper.

'Well,' crowed Shotwell, 'what does it say?'

'It says "Newmarket. 2.30. Favourite looks good".'

'Give me that!' said Shotwell, seizing the paper. 'You cheeky devil! How dare you…'

There was a knock at the door and a worried-looking custody sergeant mumbled something into Dick's ear. Dick went red and left the room.

Shotwell looked furious. 'Be some QC been sent to look after you,' he said. 'You bloody City smartarses, you're all the same.' He realised the tape recorder was still on and stopped it.

Dick came back in.

'We are releasing you,' he said to Peter.

'Oh,' said Peter. 'Why?'

'Get out!' shrieked Dick. 'Shotwell, de-arrest this man and get rid of him!'

Peter broke into a grin. 'Thank you, gentlemen,' he said. 'I will go back to the bar and finish my Punt e mes…' But, fortunately for his palate, he decided that instead he should have a word with Sir Richard… This would be an adventure to tell someone. Jane, perhaps, when she had cooled down?

'Peter, my lad, terribly sorry about this morning. Dreadful experience for you. Here, have swig of this,' and M-L pushed towards him a small tumbler, filled it full of something golden from an expensive looking bottle, and then filled a tumbler for himself.

It was worse than the Punt e mes. Peter spluttered at the force of it, the concept of 'fire water' finally meaning something to him.

'Ah,' said M-L, 'you need a little water'. He quickly left the office and came back with two plastic cups from the dispenser. 'Try half and half,' he said. 'Don't worry, most people don't like caviar first time either'.

The diluted brew actually tasted rather good, if rather hot. 'Fifteen-year-old,' said ML.

'Fifteen-year-old what?' queried Peter.

'Whisky!' said M-L. 'Gods, youth of today ain't half innocent in some directions, even if not in others...' He poured himself another half tumbler and filled the rest with water. 'Now, as I was saying, sorry about this morning, and you probably wonder what was in the envelope Miranda told you to get rid of. Well…

'Ollie Bumser and I are old mates. He ran a big operation in Germany before he settled in London. You've probably heard of his firm, OB Securities. Ollie I used to chat together every morning about the market, but you just can't do that any more. Every bloody phone call is recorded, every email is saved in perpetuity, every time you even fart someone ticks a box. And as for lighting up…

'Ollie and I needed to keep in touch – he'd have good ideas, I'd have good ideas, sometimes we felt the market had got things badly wrong and we'd throw everything we'd got at it. It was good for us, it was good for the market. We used to meet for coffee in that little place where the Deputy Governor of the Bank and the Government Broker used to get together. They always spent fifteen minutes over coffee, and when it was only ten, we knew an interest rate rise was on its way. But I digress…

'Anyway, the only way to keep in touch was to meet after business in a crowded bar, or pass on information some other way. We needed lines of communication, just weekly ones, though. And that's where you came in. Oh, and by the way, it's my niece you meet every Friday. She works for Ollie. Smart cookie, she obviously had a plan for emergencies, and it clearly worked a treat. The silly thing is, I'd nothing to say to Ollie this week, so I scrawled something like "seen any good stockings recently?" You're one of the few people who'd get that one nowadays. Ollie sent me replies via a different route. No need to tell you about those, just in case the boys in blue start asking more questions. But what gets me is, how the hell did they get onto this? Must be an insider somewhere. Well it wasn't me, and it obviously wasn't you. And it sure wasn't Miranda. Who the hell was it? Keep your ears and eyes open, Peter. We need to be on guard.'

'Yes, M-L,' said Peter, 'we certainly do'.

It was 6.45 the following Monday morning, Peter was already half way through his breakfast, when the doorbell rang. Funny, he thought. Who on earth can that be?

He opened the door.

'Peter Thistlethwaite?'

'Yes.' Good lord, it was Acting Detective Inspector Shotwell!

'Hello,' said Peter. 'Have you come to apologise?'

'No,' said Shotwell, 'we have come to arrest you for sexual assault.'

'What!' gasped Peter. 'This is some joke. Arrest *me* for assault? You really have got to be joking!'

'Alas, no,' said Dick, for he too was lurking in the background. 'Do you know someone by the name of Jane Hart?'

'Jane…' said Peter.

'And did you, on the night of Thursday 1 October touch her sexually without her consent?'

'Eh?' said Peter. 'But… but… she…'

'I am arresting you,' said Shotwell, 'for touching a woman without her consent on the evening of Thursday 1 October contrary to the Sexual Offences Act Section III. You do not have to say anything…'

The same cell. The same sensation of bewilderment. Where had it all gone wrong? The door opened.

'Now then,' said Shotwell, 'come along with me.'

It was the same interview room. The same question about wanting a solicitor. The same pained tone about it being at public expense.

'No, thank you,' said Peter. 'I am completely and utterly innocent. I would never touch a woman unless I thought I had her consent.'

'Hohoho, that's not what we heard,' said Dick. 'Interview him, Shotwell!'

'This will be easy,' said Shotwell. 'We have a first-class and wholly reliable witness who has made this complaint. She is a public servant, a member of the Inland Revenue, no less! By the way, what would you like me to call you? Shall I call you Peter?'

'Call me what you like.'

'Thank you, Peter. Now, then, Peter, did you lure Miss Jane Hart back to your apartment on the night of 1 October?'

'Er, yes, I did invite her back after we had…but hang on, no! She invited herself back!'

'Don't get carried away with ridiculous excuses,' said Shotwell. 'Not when we are getting somewhere. Now, tell me: did you offer her an amazingly strong gin and tonic?'

'Well, I suppose so, I said how much would you….'

'Enough,' said Shotwell. 'I know your type. So let's summarise so far: you lured Ms Hart back to your luxurious penthouse and plied her with strong drink. Now, what strength was the drink? You might as well come clean, because I believe it was very expensive and I intend to check it myself.'

'Er, I don't know, I think it was 47 degrees, I just asked for the very best.'

'Now we are *really* getting somewhere,' said Shotwell. '47 degrees! That's full export strength! And it costs a fortune! Did it never cross your mind that you were plying a young woman with the strongest gin available in London? You were simply intent on getting her in drink so that you could have your wicked way with her, weren't you! I know your type. Did you ply a woman with drink the last time you had sexual intercourse?'

'Er, well actually, I think you could say she plied me,' said Peter. 'But she was a barmaid, so I think she knew what she was doing.'

'You disgusting, cynical man,' said Shotwell. 'A harmless barmaid! I know your type! Picking up anyone you can lay your hands on, you don't think twice about assaulting poor young women half your size.'

'Actually,' said Peter, 'I think Jane is a bit taller than me...'

'Get on with the interview,' said Dick. 'Go on to the shocking details of tearing her clothes off.'

'Ah,' said Shotwell. 'Yes. My sense of modesty leaves me gasping here. Now then... Peter, tell me what you did after you gave Ms Hart a drink.'

'Well, I... I put my hand round her shoulder and pointed out the sights from my window.'

'You put your hand round her shoulder! And was there any need whatsoever for you to do that so that you could "show her the sights", as you put it? And what sights did you show her?'

'Well, I pointed out the Gherkin...'

'The Gherkin!' said Dick. 'Well, blow me! What sort of a dirty mind do we have here? Is there a more obviously phallic symbol in the whole of the City of London? Sorry,' he said to Shotwell, 'but I am simply appalled by what we are hearing.'

'We ain't heard nothing yet, I fear,' said Shotwell. 'Tell us what you did next.'

'Er... I... I complimented her on her earrings and then I said her eyes reminded me of a line from Ovid.'

'From where?' said Shotwell. 'Some dirty magazine I haven't come across, by the sound of it, and I've had to read quite a few in my time. This one really must be filthy if I haven't come across it... Then what did you do?'

'I... undid the top button of her blouse.'

'Aha,' said Shotwell. 'And then?'

'I undid the second button, since she hadn't objected at all to the first…'

'Just a minute, just a minute, let's stop there,' said Dick. 'How do you know she hadn't objected? Here we've got a poor frightened creature, lured into a City penthouse, she's scared, she's been plied with drink, she doesn't want to make a scene, so she suffers it all in silence. Poor thing. Let me quote from her statement here: "Peter came over to me with a… lass… a vicious look on his face". What do you make of that?'

'A vicious look? What! I don't believe it! How can she have thought…'

'Never mind. What did you do next?'

'I… undid the other buttons and slipped her top off.'

'Oh listen to this!' snorted Shotwell, 'this is the voice of a serial seducer, "slipped her top off", oh yes, now I've heard it all. You'll be telling me next you…' Dick gave him a kick. 'What did you do next?'

'I… I…'

'Come on, we know what you did, so you might as well tell us.'

'I unzipped her skirt and… it fell down.'

'Fell down! Fell down!' Shotwell and Dick were creasing themselves with unsuppressed glee. 'Just fell down, just like that! Hohoho! And then what?'

'I…I…'

'We know!'

'I pulled her tights down a little way.'

'A little way! A little way! You exposed her entirely down to her knees, did you not?'

'No, I didn't get quite that far…'

'And you were just about to brutally rip off her knickers when she gathered all her strength and bravely pushed you away.'

'She hit me on the head with her tumbler.'

'I should hope she did! Poor thing.'

'Now then, what gave you the impression she wanted any of this lewd behaviour from you? Was she saying "come on, please undo my buttons, please take off my top, please unzip my skirt"?'.

'Well, no, but she didn't say anything to discourage me.'

'Didn't she? How did she react to all your dirty talk about lines from... Ovid? Did she say oh yes, that's great, tell me more? In fact, what was her entire conversation about during the whole distressing episode? It was about *work*, was it not? She talked the whole time about your work, did she not?'

'Yes, gosh, you're right. She did.'

'Of course we're right! She tried to keep the conversation on a purely business level, but you completely ignored that, you just kept on having your wicked way. Well, Temporary Chief Inspector, I think we've got a full confession, haven't we?'

'Absolutely.' said the TCI. 'I've never seen a case quite as open and shut as this. If I were you I'd plead guilty and get a third off the sentence for coming clean. If you deny it all and go to the Crown Court you'll end up guilty, that's for sure. Juries around here don't like big bonus, gin-drinking, penthouse-living child molesters around here.'

'I'd like a solicitor,' said Peter.

'Too late,' said Dick. 'Interview is over. Switch off the tape, Acting Detective Inspector. I think we have saved the City of London from a nasty sex maniac with this highly successful interview. Let me congratulate you on it. I am sure you will be losing that *Acting* part of your title pretty soon!'

'Thank you sir, and thank you for your most constructive assistance. And may I say, sir, that your *Temporary* title must surely be a thing of the past after your equally fine support. And you, Thistlethwaite, we are releasing you on police bail. You will be up before the magistrates next. God help you, you miserable pervert.'

'Oh,' said Dick suddenly, 'charge him properly and see whether he dares to say he's innocent!'

'Ah indeed,' said Shotwell, 'thank you for reminding

me that we do things absolutely by the book in this station.'

He adopted his serious tone of voice.

'Peter Thistlethwaite, I am charging you with touching a woman sexually, knowing that you did not have her consent. How do you plead?'

'Could you repeat the last part of that?' asked Peter.

Shotwell looked confused.

'Er… knowing you did not have her consent.'

'Bollocks!' said Peter, to his immense surprise and that of the police officers. They looked quite shocked.

'Not guilty!'

Chapter Ten

'Oh Lord,' said the solicitor. 'When I was a lad... but in this day and age... you've got to get permission in triplicate before you penetrate your wife... The cases I get nowadays... Never mind, let's go through it carefully. Section III. Ah yes. Very straightforward – you've got to touch her.'

'I suppose there's no doubt about that,' said Peter.

'You've got to touch her sexually – whatever that might mean – '

'Er... yes, I suppose so, although on reflection I only touched her clothes,' said Peter.

'Interesting point,' said the solicitor, 'but let's not raise technicalities, we don't want it going to the Lords, do we... Now where was I? Ah yes. You've got to think she didn't want you to touch her.'

'Of course I thought she wanted me to touch her! And well, if she didn't, why didn't she say no, or why didn't she move away, or why didn't she leave or...'

'Ah,' said the solicitor, 'when I was a lad... but... nowadays... modern man is expected to... understand what women want. Even Freud could never work that one out, but modern man is supposed to, God help us. Let's see what the learned barrister says.'

'Oh Lord,' said the barrister. 'Absolutely ludicrous! In the good old days a woman would just give you a slap on the face,' he rubbed his check tenderly, 'but in these enlightened times a woman just slings you in the dock... Section III, I know, is really about whether you thought she was up for it... but actually it all hinges on how well the judge pushes the law and how well the jury understand what the judge says and what the jury think of young lads doing what young lads were meant to do... It's pretty clear to me you had no idea she wasn't keen, but some clever QC on the other side will argue that someone as intelligent as you should have realised she wasn't in the least bit interested. I can just see the line coming: "Every intelligent man should know what a woman doesn't want".'

'Oh, groan,' said Peter. 'Why isn't half the male population behind bars?'

'It soon will be at this rate,' said the Barrister. 'Let's just hope for an all-male jury who have been clubbing the night before. And let's hope for a judge from the old school. As long as it's not old Badger. His appalling wife tells him what to do in every sex case. At least that's what she tells everyone at dinner.'

The day arrived.

Judge Badger was sitting. The Barrister raised his eyes to heaven.

Ten of the jury were women. The Barrister gave a loud groan.

'A case is never lost till it's won,' he reassured Peter. 'My learned friend on the other side might yet cock it up.'

His learned friend rose.

'Rarely have I seen such a disgusting display of male sexual aggression,' he declared. 'This *animal* whom we see before us lured a helpless young woman, only just out of university, into his luxury apartment, plied her with very strong drink and proceeded to behave in a way which you, ladies and… ladies of the jury, may find extremely distressing. The Crown will seek to prove, nay, the Crown *will* prove, that this… this… *apparently* harmless City trader deliberately ignored *all* the signs and signals given by this poor young woman and proceeded to strip her virtually naked… *strip her virtually naked…*' he added in a louder voice, 'for a purpose which we can all too well imagine.'

'Thank you, Mr Pratt,' said the Judge. 'Mr Hope, will you proceed for the… er… defence?'

'Your Honour,' said Mr Hope,' this poor, inexperienced young man got a little carried away after an exciting evening's conversation with a woman whom he had known for some time; he had no indication whatsoever that his behaviour was in any way unwelcome. The Defence will prove that his actions were tender and emotionally appreciative, inspired by the beauty of this young, but nevertheless mature woman, a highly educated member of society and a member, in addition, of Her Majesty's Inland Revenue, not an institution renowned for recruiting those who are soft of heart and emotionally incapable of defending themselves, but those who are tough, rigorous, alert.'

'Wow,' thought Peter. 'Not bad!'

The Badger looked dismayed, but then he looked at the public gallery. It was full of tough-looking young women. He looked at the Press Gallery. Full of tough-looking young women. He looked at the jury… He smiled.

'Please proceed with your first witness,' he said to the Prosecution, who looked in need of some tender and appreciative action from any woman not known for her toughness.

Jane entered the witness box, handkerchief in hand.

'If you would need a break at any time, please do not hesitate to ask for one,' said the Badger gently.

'Thank you, your Honour,' said Jane, 'that is exceptionally kind of you. Thank you for noticing how distressed I am.'

The Badger smiled.

'Now then, Miss Hart,' said the Prosecution. 'I am sorry to have to ask you to recount your ordeal at the hands, and I fear I must repeat, at the *hands* of this lascivious City Trader.'

'Your Honour,' said Jane. 'I knew Mr Thistlethwaite at College. We went to meetings of the Modern Theological Society together. I thought he was totally trustworthy, I thought I was safe in his company. I knew he had been sent down for gross moral turpitude, but I thought there had possibly been a mistake. How wrong I was…' she blew her nose.

'Gross moral turpitude!' exclaimed the Badger,

grasping his pen with vigour. 'Gross moral turpitude! Well, well, well! Now I have heard it all! Please continue if you feel you are able to…'

'When I got my job he invited me to dinner in an expensive restaurant and ordered a very expensive bottle of strong wine. He then…' she blew her nose again. 'He then… pressed me to come to his luxury penthouse pretending the view was the best in London. Then he…' she blew her nose again.

'Would you like a break?' asked the Badger.

'Thank you, your Honour,' said Jane, 'but I must get through this ordeal as soon as I can.'

'Very good,' said the Badger, 'I admire your courage.'

'When we entered his apartment he immediately pulled off my coat and offered me more drink. I felt it would be impolite to refuse. He then showed me the awful view, putting his arm tightly round my shoulder. I felt it would be impolite to brush it off – I have always been brought up to be polite – so I started talking about his work. He forced me to drink an expensive, very, very strong gin with hardly any tonic and then, before I knew it, he began to unbutton my blouse. He was so practised that I barely realised what he was doing. I kept desperately talking about work, not realising he was intent on…' she began to cry… 'on taking off my blouse, which he did, it was so casual he must have done it *hundreds* of times before to equally innocent young women, and then he pulled me to him and I was scared out of my life and I kept desperately talking about work and he then put his hand on the zip of my skirt and before I knew what had happened my skirt was on the floor and he had pulled my tights down to my knees and I was shocked and horrified and frightened and…' she sobbed loudly… 'thought I would be raped so I hit him on the head with my tumbler and ran.'

'You have done very well,' said the Badger. 'Do have a break!'

'No, your Honour,' said Jane, I will see this through!'

'Well done,' said the Badger. 'I hope the Defence will

be brief.'

Mr Hope rose with difficulty.

'Ms Hart,' he said, 'do you have much experience with young men?'

'Your Honour,' screamed the Prosecution, 'I feel such questioning is totally inappropriate!'

'I was about to make the same point myself,' said the Badger.

'Very well,' said the Defence. 'Ms Hart, how many times in your life have you made it clear to a man that you did not want his attentions?'

'Your Honour!' exclaimed the Prosecution...

'Absolutely,' said the Badger. 'I should be grateful if the Defence could focus on the facts'.

'Very well,' said the Defence. 'Miss Hart. Before you hit the defendant viciously on the head, had you made it clear you did not want his attentions?'

Jane sobbed loudly. 'Your Honour,' she said... 'if... that *rake* did not realise I *loathed* his attentions, he must be... he must be... sick in the head!'

'Thank you very much,' said the Badger. 'Does that conclude the case for the Defence?'

'But your Honour,' said the Defence, 'I have only just started.'

'It strikes me,' said the Badger, 'that your cross examining is not doing your client any good whatsoever in the eyes of the members of the jury and that this young lady needs to be able to stand down.'

For good measure, Jane gave an extra-loud sniff.

'Very well,' said the Defence. 'I suppose we shall need to pass on to the defendant.'

Peter got out of the Dock and crawled to the stand. He didn't feel good. He had just had an insight. He now realised what all Jane's talk about 'work' had been for. What an absolute idiot he'd been! Jane had simply asked him about what he did that might incriminate M-L. And as soon as she'd got what she wanted about Friday, she'd hit him on the head. She hadn't been interested in him at all!

He couldn't believe it. But it was all completely clear now. Why hadn't he seen it before? Jane, the Scholar, his previous idol, couldn't care less about him! She'd used him! Or maybe the Revenue had been using her! Yes, it was all clear now. He groaned.

'Please do not groan,' said the Badger. 'Or do you wish to change your plea, having realised the weakness of your case?'

'No, sir,' said Peter.

'I am addressed as "your Honour", kindly bear that in mind. A man of your supposed intelligence should know better.

'Mr Hope, please get on with your case. I am sure you will not need long with this witness.'

'No indeed, your Honour,' said the Hope, 'I am sure I can swiftly prove that my client is completely innocent.'

The Badger failed to conceal a malicious grin. He had a curious moustache, which was something of a cross between those of Charlie Chaplin and Adolf Hitler.

'Mr Thistlethwaite,' said the Hope, 'did Ms Hart give you any idea she did not welcome your advances?'

'None whatsoever. Looking back at it now, I realise she simply wanted to get some information out of me, and as soon as she'd got it, she hit me.'

'Some information?' interrupted the Badger. 'What information?'

'She wanted to get some information so that my boss could be accused of insider dealing.'

Mr Hope groaned. The Public Gallery shot upright. The Press Gallery scribbled faster.

'Insider dealing!' mused the Badger grabbing his pen. 'Insider dealing. Well, well, well. Now I really have heard it all. Have you finished, Mr Hope? Your client, if I may say so, is not assisting your case.'

'I'm sorry, your Honour, this is new to me, but it does seem perfectly clear that the defendant had no idea whatsoever that his advances were unwelcome.'

'Thank you,' said the Badger, 'I think it is time for Mr

Pratt to start his cross examination.'

The Pratt leapt to his feet and gave a little backwards kick in anticipation.

'Mr Thistlethwaite,' he said. 'How many innocent young women have you lured to your apartment?'

'None,' said Peter.

'Mr Thistlethwaite,' said the Pratt, 'in your statement to the police you admitted that you had recently lured a *barmaid* to your luxury penthouse, did you not?'

Squawks of disgust from the Public Gallery. One of the Press women rushed out.

'Well, yes, but…'

'I repeat my question: how many innocent young women have you slept with?'

'None.'

'And you seriously expect the ladies… the members of the jury to believe that??'

Several more Press reporters rushed in. The Gallery was overflowing. Peter groaned.

'Are you sure you would not like to change your plea?' asked the Badger in a tired voice.

'No… I honestly had no idea she wasn't interested, that she was using me…'

'Mr Thistlethwaite,' said the Badger, 'you must be extremely careful in the accusations you are now making.'

The Pratt beamed. 'Thank you, your Honour. Quite honestly, having heard what I have, I feel I have absolutely no need to ask any further questions whatsoever.'

'Nor have I anything more to ask, your Honour,' said Mr Hope in a weary voice. 'I think that probably concludes the case for the Defence.'

The final speeches were brief. It was not long before the Judge was summing up. Just before he did so, a rather formidable-looking woman boldly entered the court. The court usher immediately rushed up and escorted her to a seat at the very front of the public gallery. The Badger smiled deferentially while all this was going on, and continued only when she had made herself comfortable.

The Badger then began to muse in a loud voice.

'Members of the jury,' he said, 'you must decide whether this fast-living insider-dealing City trader lured this defenceless young child to his *de luxe* city penthouse, plied her with strong drink and proceeded to have his wicked way with her until she mustered all her confidence and courageously pushed him away – or' (as something of an aside) 'whether he did not.' In a louder voice, 'You must decide whether she gave any impression whatsoever she wanted this lewd, morally turpitudinous, lecherous, barmaid-seducing villain stripping off her clothing… or,' in a whisper, 'not.'

Peter groaned. Mr Hope groaned. Mr Pratt kicked his foot backwards. The woman at the front of the public gallery smiled and gave an appreciative nod. The Badger relaxed in relief.

The Jury took three minutes.

Peter got six months.

'Well, well, a right toff we've got here, then!' said the Chief Warder. 'And a filthy one! Sexual assault and you got six months! Nice bit of assaulting that must have been, then! Cor, I just like to think how far you got, you lucky beggar. Disgusting. Mind, you're in good company here. The shrink will see you first, and then it's the guvnor. What a pair. God help you. Hope you like your new outfit.'

Peter found his new clothes a bit of a contrast with what he had now become accustomed to wearing, but they weren't quite as rough as the outfit he'd had to wear at school.

'Wait your turn here,' said the Warder, leading him down a passageway.

'Bloody waste of time this interview, I can tell you. Anyone can see you're as far from suicidal as I am from a hot dinner. All you're interested in is getting out as soon as you can to pursue your wicked way again. Disgusting!'

Peter sat down in one of the padded chairs in the waiting room and looked at the picture on the wall. 'What do you make of this?' was the caption. Funny title. He looked at the painting itself. Abstract, of course. The bottom bit looked like an animal with horns and with something dropping from its rear end. Above there were a lot of squiggly lines. Peter concentrated. Hmmm. Could that be a female body... was that a male... oops! And what was that big circle supposed to be? He was just getting into it when a voice called out.

'Next, please!'

He walked in the direction of the voice and found a door open. There was a man in a white coat behind it wearing thick-rimmed glasses and a floppy bow tie.

'Hello, one and a half!'

'Good god! Psycho! What are you doing here? And why are you so different?'

'Ah, events, dear boy, events. New job demands a new image, you know, and I'd never have got this one if I hadn't played the appropriate role. It doesn't pay all that badly, and it's great for the cv. And for what I learn here too, by gad! I could rewrite a few textbooks now, that's for sure! I wonder how Freud would have come out if he'd worked in Vienna Gaol on a load of tough young men rather than in the posh suburbs with genteel Jewish women?'

'So you chose to come here?'

'Get real! No, bit of a sad tale, really. I was doing really well with all my City contacts, and I even had one day a week in Harley Street, megabucks, I tell you, and my speciality was frustrated females. Then I had this rather genteel bit of stuff, poor woman, whose husband was working all hours of the day and night and so when he got to bed all he really wanted was a bit of shut-eye. My listening to her for hours wasn't doing much good, it was him I needed to talk to – don't you believe all that guff about the presenting patient being the problem – anyway, one day I felt so sorry for her that I gave her a bit of alternative therapy and achieved more in ten minutes than I'd done in ten weeks.'

Psycho smiled nostalgically.

'Trouble was, though, that once she'd had the real thing she started having a proper go at her husband, and that only made things worse of course, so she told him he needed to see a proper psycho and she'd give him a damn good address and then, of course, he started putting two together and she let slip a thing or two and... I didn't know that her hubby was the principal of a bloody royal college, I should have recognised the name, but...

'He couldn't get me professionally, of course, it would have reflected pretty badly on him, so he just made sure I didn't get my Harley Street room renewed, and then he made trouble with my other premises, and...

'Look, if you ever need any weed, just say you need to see me 'cos you've had a sighting of the Virgin Mary and I'll make sure you get something good...'

'Thanks,' said Peter, 'that's very kind. I'm trying to think of when I last saw you, and it must have been the firm's Christmas Party... Did you...er... go on anywhere interesting after it?'

'Oh lord!' said Psycho. 'I won't forget that in a hurry! What a cock up it was. You remember that girl with the crucifix, nice bit of fluff, but what a mess she ended me up with. I couldn't get rid of her at the end, she was clinging to me like a limpet, so with enormous reluctance I took her home, and told her to make herself comfortable on my bed while I had a quick shower and blow me, what do I find when I get out of the bathroom? She's thrown up all over the place and done a runner! Took me most of the next morning to clear it all up. I ask you!'

'I see,' said Peter, suppressing a smile with great difficulty. 'Still, what do you expect from a crucifix?'

'Well,' said the Governor, 'I don't see every new prisoner, of course, but someone from St B's... gods, what a frustrating time I had there! It's mixed now, isn't it, a willing woman on every staircase? Gods, I wish I could have my time all over again. Now then, an educated man like you must *educate*! I'm all in favour of education, education, education, as one of our lords and masters used to say. So if you are any good I'll give you a classroom, and in the meanwhile you must decide on something to teach these poor devils. If we could get *one* of them through a GCSE, I'd get an OBE! What could you teach?'

'Er, perhaps some Latin?' suggested Peter. 'No… er… some Ancient History? No. Some… basic Greek? Or could I start with something like… oh yes, how the stock market works? If they could learn how to make money without violence, that might be useful…?'

'What an excellent idea!' said the Governor. 'Let us try you out on that. It will be a great line for the Minister. Let me write it down. And I will come along myself. "Money without violence." Splendid! The Minister may be able to use it in the House.'

The next day Peter was in his new classroom. Half the members of the audience seemed to be warders. The other half didn't exactly look as if they were inside for insider dealing.

'Now,' said Peter confidently. 'Why work for your money when you can make your money work for you?'

There were big nods of the head and grunts of approval all round. The Governor looked pleased.

'Yes,' said Peter, 'if you pick the right share to invest in, you can double your money *and* get a dividend. A dividend,' he quickly added, 'is a cheque twice a year. I mean free *money* twice a year.' The atmosphere was getting even better.

'So,' said Peter, 'let us say I invest… one hundred pounds in… *Group 5*, that's the company that runs a few prisons. Do you think they make a good profit? Of course they do. Look at the way they treat prisoners… in prisons which are run by them,' he added quickly. 'Of course they make a damn good profit! Why, their share price rose twenty per cent last year… I mean if you had invested a hundred pounds at the beginning of the year, you'd have got two dividends as well as having a share worth twenty pounds more than you bought it for.' The warders were nodding their heads thoughtfully. The Governor also looked pensive.

'This is a damn good talk,' he said to the room. 'Damn sight better than the one last week, that vicar – with the same name as you, curiously, on eternal forgiveness.' Grunts all round. 'Any questions?' he asked, 'or can we let Mr Thistlethwaite go on?'

'Just a minute,' said one of the inmates. 'How do we know which companies to put our money in apart from *Group 5*? My brother-in-law has a friend who says he lost his shirt by investing in something called Maxwell. I think it was coffee.'

'Ah, yes,' said Peter. 'A bad business that was. But what a very good question! Well,' he said, 'you just ask someone on the inside, like me! I can tell you! Or,' he added, with a twinkle in his eye, 'you set up your own company! Get a loan from the bank, in fact the government will often give you a free loan too, set yourself up, and if it all goes wrong you just declare yourself bankrupt and start all over again! But if it all goes right…' he paused for effect, 'you become a millionaire!'

The class was buzzing a bit too loudly, so the Governor decided to take things down a little.

'Very good,' he said, 'but a bit idealistic! What sort of company could these lads set up? You must be realistic, Thistlethwaite!'

'Of course,' said Peter. 'Let me think. How about this…

'Everyone in this room is, of course, very experienced in their dealings with women.'

There was a bit of shuffling, but enough grunts and nods and *you bets* to continue. 'But,' said Peter, 'not everyone is. In fact, when I went to university, I'd never kissed a woman in my life.'

'Er... very interesting,' said the Governor, 'but what's this got to do with setting up a company?'

'Everything,' said Peter. 'You see, what I needed was a company that would help me. Not a simple dating agency, that's for people who know what they're doing. No, what I needed was a company for complete innocents, one that would tell me the right way to invite a girl for a glass of sherry. How to say nice things to her, the sort of things a woman likes to hear. How to give her a kiss. How to give her compliments and then put your arm around her, how to undo her top button without her being bothered, how to...'

'Alright, alright,' said the Governor, a little out of breath. 'Keep it to the financial side, please.'

'Well,' said Peter, 'I think there is an urgent need for a company like this to be set up. And you wouldn't need much to do it. Why, a nice room to explain things to people, a few experienced young lads like you to do this explaining, maybe a few nice girls as well, remember, these will be poor innocent young men who need help... and you would advertise it through tasteful little cards and leaflets, you could set up a website, you could...' he was really getting into the swing of it now... 'then expand and have a parallel company *teaching young girls how to behave when they met young men for the first time*! We'd need lots of experienced men to tell them what to do, probably men like you, and we'd probably have to have an advanced section for girls who really wanted to get laid and wanted to know all about it...and we'd hand out leaflets outside all the girls' schools, especially the convent schools...'

The Governor wanted to intercede, but he saw the audience in the room wouldn't take kindly to it.

'And then, when people saw what a great success it was in one town, we'd take it to another, and another, and then we'd have one in every big city in England, and Wales, and Scotland... and then we'd go global, Europe, the States, and there are lots of terribly innocent young women in Japan, and in Singapore the birth-rate is falling because men and women are waiting longer and longer to get married and suddenly find they can't speak the same sexual language, and did you know that seventy per cent of young men in Spain have their first sexual experience with a prostitute? There's a market for you! And we'd call this company *First Time*, and it would be first rate, and we'd all make a lot of money!

There was uproar. The Governor took a long time to calm things down. 'Damn good talk,' he said. 'Damn good. You know, I think this idea is… really not quite as foolish as it might appear, and when I think back to my own youth, I certainly… I mean I can think of several people of my acquaintance who could have benefited from such an organisation…'

The next day Peter had his own cell. He had some strange small black pellets on his smoked salmon, but they tasted as bad as Punt e mes. He handed out tips, he drafted the memorandum for a new company, he was besieged by anxious young men wanting to become investors in *First Time*, escorts for *First Time*, men whose sisters were desperate to get jobs with *First Time*… the Governor informed him that the Minister, a bachelor, thought his scheme was a brainwave which even the Opposition couldn't have come up with, and he himself would be delighted to have a seat on the Board of any company that might be set up once he had been obliged to step down as Minister, which could be quite soon… But the euphoria only lasted a week, because very strange things had happened in the City. The Badger had got arrested for sexually assaulting an apparently very unwilling barmaid behind a downstairs bar in Bishopsgate, and whatever the Badger might say about having his drink spiked and the barmaid initially seeming very willing indeed, Mr Hope made it abundantly clear that a judge who did this sort of thing in his private life clearly could not judge *anyone* in sexual matters. Mr Pratt too had had a few problems. He claimed he had been pulled into a back alley where some of a pretty redhead's clothes were already on the ground and she had started screaming; but several passers-by, highly respectable men from the City, claimed to have seen a very different sequence of events. Oh my goodness, who would have believed that the apparently upright Mr Pratt could have done this sort of thing in broad daylight! A deal seemed to have been reached surprisingly quickly, and Mr Pratt immediately withdrew his endorsement of the pronouncements of Judge Badger on matters sexual, and in a matter of days the Badger's recent relevant judgements were all declared unsafe.

Things did not end there. The Gods seemed to have realised they had given Peter a remarkably bad hand, and he soon received the news that Acting Inspector Shotwell had suddenly reverted to plain Sergeant, while the Temporary Chief Inspector was back to plain Inspector. And to cap it all, poor Jane had also been a victim of the Gods' displeasure, for she had been summarily dismissed from the Revenue for claiming her boss had made a pass at her. Well, well.

Peter left the prison to cheers and sad farewells.

A Rolls-Royce was waiting for him.

'Sorry it took so long,' said M-L, 'but it's pretty well all sewn up now. 'Bastards, the lot of them.'

'Are you alright?' said a pretty redhead.

'Friday!' said Peter! 'Gods, I couldn't half do with a G and T.' 'Here you are,' said M-L, opening the mini-fridge. 'Miranda, do the ice and lemon bit, will you? I think I'll pour myself a little whisky.'

'M-L,' said Peter, 'you know you once said I could call in a favour any time'.

'Er, didn't I just do one for you?'

'Oh,' said Peter... 'yes... thank you... but do you think you and your pals could get me a few papers together so that I could get back to St B's in a different guise? I'd really like to start all over again... But before that, I'd also like to set up a new company...'

Chapter Eleven

Raising funds for *First Time* was not exactly difficult. Who knew that the 'eminent prison Governor with a passion for reform' was actually a frustrated bumbling oaf hoping for a few thrills on the side? Who could have known that one of the biggest potential sponsors was anxious to use the acceptable face of innocent dating for the very less than acceptable face which he practised in his clubs down back alleys?

'Sprats for mackerel,' declared M-L, 'but we've gotta have them. Some of them have got more money than sense, but some of them are actually quite sensible. Let's face it, though, if they had no sense at all they'd be working for the Revenue or the CPS or,' and he guffawed, 'the FSA!'

The room was full. Peter was quite nervous as he took his place alongside M-L on the podium. 'Don't worry,' said M-L. 'Full room is the easiest. It's the half-full ones that are the problem. Now then, shall we get going? Best to start with a joke which might have an element of truth in it...

'Morning everyone!' he bellowed, reducing the hubbub to immediate silence. 'And blow me, don't I see every one of the most experienced men – and women,' he added, with a deferential nod towards the only woman in the room '– in the City before me! Yet all of us started off, I'm sure, in the most uncomfortable and unpromising situations imaginable, quick kiss in the back lane, quick grope behind the bike sheds, and then, wonder of wonders, back row of the cinema... ah, youth, what a... I mean what an appalling time we all had to start with, and now, blow me, where are we all today? Yes, we made it, we were the successful ones, but think of all those poor sods, I mean,' again with a deferential nod towards the woman, a very attractive blonde with flowing curly locks and a brighter than usual scarf on her standard suit, 'think of all those poor young things who found it… difficult to find the bike sheds or the back lane or… nowadays, I have no doubt, to find the dark bit in the night club where you can have a quick snog or 'pull' or whatever it is they call it, ah yes, we have a moral duty to help those less fortunate than ourselves to find fulfilment and happiness and… and… the service to the community is unimaginable, why, I need only quote the words of Reginald Scrub, OBE, Governor of one of Her Majesty's major prisons and who has generously agreed to join our Board of Directors, why, Mr Scrub has claimed that more than half of his inmates for sex offences would not be inside if they had had the privilege of what we intend to offer, while Sir Hugh Hifner, who has also agreed to join the Board, sees our enterprise as something invaluable in the progress of youth towards the more adult world in which he traditionally operates. I am sure you have all seen our website, and the documentation which outlines our growth aims and prospects, and so I would now like to hand you over to the prospective CEO of our proposed company, a man of immense talent, enthusiasm and industry, Peter Thistlethwaite!'

There was a generous round of applause as M-L sat down and gulped a large mouthful of the water-coloured liquid in his glass. 'Aaaah,' he whispered to Peter, 'if you've got to force vodka down, make sure you have the best…'.

Peter rose. He felt important. He reached over and helped himself to a small mouthful of M-L's glass. The best? He'd never had anything like this before.

'Sir Richard' he declaimed confidently, 'is one of the most colourful characters in the City, and if he deems an enterprise worthy of following, it will be either dismal failure or, much more likely, a magnificent success! As he has suggested, every beginning is difficult. We all probably have to start in the bottom league and move slowly up the tables until we might make it into the top. But it's not exactly easy. And for some it's so frightening that they daren't even start. That's where we come in.

'Do you know how Brigitte Bardot responded to the question "how did you lose your virginity?" "Beautifully," she apparently said! Well, she was either lying big-time or, like me, she had the most immense stroke of luck. Because, without luck, I wouldn't have had a hope! Why? Because my father was a vicar. Because my mother was a vicar's wife. Because I went to a single sex school. But like B.B., I still lost my virginity beautifully. How? Because I was taken in hand by two gentle, patient teachers who taught me how to do everything necessary to get it right! Not just how to do the real thing – and by god the second teacher was good at that! – but how to build up to it, how to flatter a woman, how to make her really interested in you, how to say the right things and do the right things so that you can charm the pants off her' – the blonde with the bright scarf had suddenly gone rather bright herself, and Peter felt flustered – 'if she really wants them charmed off, of course', he added, 'and build the basis for a really good relationship!

'Now is it just the English who are so bad at this? Can we learn anything from other countries… from, say, Germany?'

A big blond-haired man in the second row leaned earnestly forward.

'We can learn a lot,' said Peter, 'and we must build on what they can do. Did you know that all Germans from good families go to so-called "dancing lessons" when they are in their early teens, and they learn how to ask a woman for a dance, how to dress for the occasion, how to help a woman out of and into her coat, and even… how to dance! But they're not told the really important things, and that's where we can take over. Because the Germans, god bless them, believe that sex happens naturally and simply and unproblematically, and they're quite wrong! We need schools that go to the next stage, and the one after that, and even the one after that. No pussy-footing! The young need to be taught how to kiss! And how to dress! Bright young

111

things shouldn't go around looking hungry if they haven't had the slightest bit of experience. That leads to them getting too much attention and enough gropes to put them off for life. No, they need to be gently educated, through talks and lectures, and personal explanation and advice and guidance, and how to flirt, and how to say "no" politely – everyone must be brought up to be polite – and it can all be done quite inexpensively for those who are not so well off, whereas those from wealthier families can have private tuition. And our tutors, of course, will only be first-rate!'

There was full applause as Peter sat down.

'Nice!' whispered M-L. 'I must say, though, I've never been so excited as when I was behind the bike sheds, but never let pleasure get in the way of business…'

As he rose again, two men in ill-fitting suits and nondescript ties left from the back of the room, but everyone else kept in their seats. The blonde had regained her cool and was smiling warmly at Peter.

'Any questions?' asked M-L, taking a large mouthful from his glass.

The blond in the second row raised his hand. 'Zis is good,' he declared. 'You are right indeed. I too am going to dancing lessons in my youth. But you are right again indeed. What are they teaching me? How to help a woman into her coat. Zis no good in London. Women equal. They not want helping into coat. They think you male chauvinist. They are laughing at you. But what I am needing to be learning is how to make pass at girl. How to make them laugh. Zis is what matters. All the other dealers can do zis, but not me. I must be learning. I must become customer. And I must invest in zis company!'

'Splendid!' said M-L, 'but I must warn you that we have already had undertakings for no less than ten million and we intend to close at fifteen.'

'Count me in for half a bar!' called out a burly figure in the front row with a very red nose, who looked as if he might have paid quite a lot of money to get it that colour.

'God knows why, but my daughter's scared stiff of men and couldn't half do with some advice of this sort. Damn good presentation, now, where are the drinks?'

'Can I ask a question?' piped up a middle-aged man near the back. 'It all sounds very sensible, but just supposing my daughter were to be registered for this, how do I know she won't end up in bed with a highly unsuitable man who's also been along to the course and who has, as you charmingly put it, charmed the pants off her?'

'Damn good point!' said M-L. 'Er… I'll let Mr Thistlethwaite answer that one.'

'We are,' said Peter, 'the answer to every parent's concern. Women will be taught how to say "no", and men will be taught that "no means no", so there will be a firm moral basis to all of this and the best families in the country will have no hesitation in sending their young men and women for advice and help and reassurance and… everyone in this room with a son or a daughter should feel comfortable in sending their offspring to *First Time*, because we are the alternative to quick gropes in the night club, to which, let's face it, they're all going to go at some point, and where some might be put off for life!'

'Excellent,' announced M-L, 'and now, if there are no further questions, we have a little light refreshment to which I, for one, would not be averse. Subscription forms are available in the foyer, some of our videos on how to kiss and… so on are also available for those who are still in the dark, hohoho, and there is a minimum subscription of ten k, and the Directors will be happy to circulate over hospitality…'

There was a further appreciative round of applause, followed by a stampede for the bar. M-L led the way. The vodka might be superb, but there was no substitute for whisky.

Peter slowly made his way out of the room, to be joined by the blonde.

'Hello,' she said, 'you won't remember me, but I was at

113

St B's. I think we may have…overlapped slightly.'

Peter looked intently at her. The golden curls were definitely something he could remember from somewhere. She blushed.

'I…just wanted to say… that… I think your company is a great idea. You see, I was pushed in at the deep end of a night club, and I don't think I ever really grasped the idea of innocent flirting for the pleasure of it, it was just a question of showing you could pull more than anyone else and…'

Peter smiled.

'Hey,' he said, 'say no more. It's dreadful that someone so obviously intelligent and sensitive and beautiful as you should have been denied genuine romance! You poor thing! And St B's probably didn't help. Oh my god!' He suddenly stared at her in semi-recognition. 'You weren't… er… you weren't by chance… a member of…'

'Yes, yes,' said the woman, going redder than ever. 'Oh lord, I'm most terribly sorry. I was responsible for it all. But I just don't believe that we thought you could be the unsexiest man in college! Gosh, you were unbelievable just now! So powerful! But you're also so… charming… and…'

'Let me get you a drink,' said Peter. 'I wish I could look at you a bit more closely, your golden locks, they remind me of… er, and your eyes… never mind… but yes, they really do… they…'

'Yes…?'

'Oh, it's silly, but they remind me of a line in Ovid, sorry, ridiculous, I know, but… there's that powerful sense in them, they're so soft and gentle and yet they're like a fire wanting to burst into flame and… I'm sorry, I'm getting a bit carried away, but… you are one of the most beautiful and charming women I have ever met! Forgive me!'

Blondilocks took Peter's hand and gave it a squeeze.

'No one's ever talked to me like that before,' she gasped. 'I now feel even worse about that dreadful

114

occasion, although we all thought it was fun until the Dean turned up. I still feel awfully guilty… if there's any way in which I can make it up for you at all…'

'There certainly is!' said Peter. 'Let me take you for a drink this evening so that I can talk you to and gaze into your beautiful eyes all night! But first let's get this hospitality over with. Can I get you… a small sherry? There's plenty of hard stuff, but the sherry is delicate. I chose it myself…'

After ten minutes M-L told Peter that they were already over-subscribed and that he might as well get back to the office. But he didn't actually get there until three hours later, after a very interesting detour via the penthouse.

'Sorry it took me so long, M-L,' he apologised, 'but I've just been signing up another tutor. Advanced cases only for her, I think. She was at St B's, of course.'

'Good old St B's!' triumphed M-L. 'That definitely calls for another whisky! Oh, by the way, haven't you got an interview at the old place soon?'

Chapter Twelve

Peter's application for a place at St Badley's looked impeccable. It was amazing what M-L's friends had managed to cobble together for him. He should have been offered a place on the strength of the application papers alone, but there were the obligatory interviews. Still, what were they? It wasn't exactly his first bash at this particular game.

An interview with the College economist was either a raging success or, more commonly, a dismal failure. The economist didn't want to have too many people to teach, it got in the way of Higher Economics. Peter was well primed, though. He knew the standard questions, even if he wasn't quite sure about the standard answers. But from what he had heard of the man, there was a simple way to get the necessary boxes ticked.

The Head Porter did not recognise him. Why should he associate that failed, poorly-dressed, self-conscious, morally turpitudinous Thistlethwaite with this dapper, wealthy, exceptionally confident public schoolboy?

'Interview with Dr Butt, sir? Yes, go straight ahead, turn right into the side court, take the big door, turn right, turn left, there's a door twenty yards on your right, go up three flights and it's the first on your left.'

Peter wondered how anyone managed to find the room, never mind get accepted.

'Thank you, my man,' he responded. 'Here's something for you,' and he handed over a coin. He delighted in the porter's embarrassment. He knew the man had probably never been given a tip in his life, and the effect was transformational. 'Sir, that is most exceptionally kind of you, but… but… I really can't accept, sir… Let me take you to Dr Butt's rooms myself!'

That was a useful bonus.

The porter, eyeing the interviewee as something of a higher being, chatted deferentially as he escorted Peter along a route the latter recalled fairly well. Nothing had changed, it seemed. Same old broken cobblestones. Same old bits of clover in the grass. Wonderful!

They ascended the stairs and the porter knocked boldy on Dr Butt's door.

'Sir, I have a Mr Thistlethwaite for interview with you, sir!'

The Butt was taken aback. This was the first occasion in thirty years that a porter had brought a candidate personally, and the Head Porter at that. And this was quite wrong. Part of the interview was finding his room on time. This would not do. Why on earth had the porter bothered? He looked at Peter and quickly realised. This interviewee was no ordinary hopeful. The suit, the tie, the cufflinks, the shoes…

'Sit down,' he said, slightly uneasily, fingering the non-existing tie around his dirty collar.

Peter surveyed the room he had occasionally heard stories about. A couple of boxes that could well have been used for potatoes from Butt's farm. Graphs of share prices strewn all over the floor. He looked at the Butt: filthy fingernails, shoes still muddy from the potato lifting, wild eyes that clearly never tolerated much sleep. How could he possibly be an Oxford don? Peter smiled. The Butt, uncertain, smiled back.

'Ah, now then, what's your name?'

The Butt never looked at applications in advance. He would never have rumbled Peter's impressive, but fake c.v. anyway. 'Go at them cold', was his motto. In other words, make life as easy as possible for yourself.

'Ah, yes, Thistlethwaite. Now then, Thistlethwaite, why do you want to study Economics?

Standard question Number One. The answer had to be unstandard, that was for sure.

'I am attracted by the large sums of money that can be made by anticipating political, and therefore economic, movements in the world, especially Emerging Markets.'

The Butt blinked.

'I see,' he said. Good. And... er... why do you want to study this subject at St Badley's?'

Standard question Number Two. Very easy to produce an unstandard answer to this.

'I understand, sir, that the fellow in charge of Economics,' he coughed slightly, 'I mean yourself, has a keen interest in the fundamentals of the Stock Market and in the valuation of companies.'

The Butt was *very* taken aback. He'd never had this before.

'Er... I see,' he said, 'er... yes..., it is true, er... thank you for your confidence...er what do you understand by "elasticity"?'

Standard question Number Three. If you ask standard questions, mate, you run the risk of not getting the best out of people...

'Elasticity is a basic concept in Economics which relates demand to price, its degree being measured by a good's desirability or necessity. It is clearly related to opportunity cost. Highly elastic goods are those in which a minor change in price produces a sharp change in demand, inelastic goods are those for which price is unrelated to the latter. In the classical model, insulin would be regarded as an 'inelastic' good, it is essential, whatever the price. But let me digress a little, you must have heard insulin mentioned by every interview candidate for the last twenty years. Let us look instead at, say...first growth clarets. Why, if you look at the price of clarets over the period 1987 to the present day, you will see the phenomenon of elasticity in perfect operation. But,' he said, in a quieter voice, knowing the Butt was slightly deaf and would have to strain to hear, '*there are significant anomalies to be found. And this is where money is to be made.* There are in fact all sorts of other anomalous examples in the stock market, as you yourself are bound to know. Why, look at the price of...' his voice trailed off.

'Yes,' said the Butt eagerly, 'what did you have in mind?'

'Well,' said Peter. 'I am sorry, I am straying from the question slightly with this... but I regularly shadow in a busy City office and I wonder whether a small piece of inside information I have might really make it impossible for me to continue. However,' he went on, in a more cheerful mode, 'there are certainly companies which regularly defy the model of "elasticity", indeed, I could probably name at least one that will rise handsomely in price before the week is out, despite the current market turbulence.'

The Butt looked very interested, but slightly sceptical.

'YL Technology,' said Peter. 'If that has not risen smartly before the end of the week, then I clearly do not deserve a place at this college.'

The Butt's eyes bounced from side to side. His large, ugly ears were almost twitching.

'Alright,' he said. 'If YLT do jump before the week is out, your place here is secure!'

'That is very kind of you, sir,' said Peter, 'but I would not want to gain a place on such a flimsy piece of information. After all, there must be many others applying who have much more to offer than me.'

'Crap,' said the Butt. 'You're the smartest I've seen in ten years! Mind you, if YLT don't bounce, I'll change my mind. Oh, and I'll need to read your papers,' he added, as an afterthought.

'I think, sir, said Peter, that we can both be quietly confident about YLT.' The Butt beamed.

The second interview proved another dream. Peter was surprised how much he could remember about what interviewers claimed they were looking for, but for what they actually probed.

'Ah, Thistlethwaite, I am the Admissions Tutor and I have to ask you some hard questions!' Big grin.

'Of course, sir, I should be disappointed if you didn't.' Surprised, but bigger grin.

'Why did you choose St Badley's?'

'A variety of reasons. A distant relation of mine was

here, and before he left, under, I am afraid, a heavy cloud, he claimed he had never enjoyed himself more, intellectually, that is, than when he was here. I too want to be intellectually challenged and motivated, and my argument with Dr Butt proved I shall very much enjoy my tutorials with him.'

'Ah, you argued with Dr B, did you? That's a very good sign. But tell me, who was this relative of yours, the name rings a bell... good lord... it wasn't the chap who was sent down for...for... gross moral turpitude, was it?'

'Ah,' said Peter, 'I clearly cannot hide anything from you! Yes, indeed, the charge seemed totally out of keeping with the character I knew. But I also knew that St Badley's prides itself on its non-discrimination policy, and it would never, never discriminate against anyone on grounds of gender, race, disability or... family.'

'Absolutely right!' shouted the Admissions Tutor. 'No discrimination! Morally wrong! And, indeed, illegal! The only thing we would discriminate against is a Public School – government policy, of course,' he emphasised, 'and you didn't go to one, did you?'

'Of course not,' said Peter. 'My poor father could never in his wildest dreams have afforded it'.

The Admissions Tutor looked at Peter's suit. He himself was dressed down. Big time. 'Er... have you nevertheless had some financial advantage at any stage of your career?'

'Well,' said Peter, lowering his voice. 'I feared this could count against me, but since you have been quite firm about not discriminating against anyone... I was bought this outfit, especially for this interview, by a rich acquaintance who,' and he dropped his voice even lower, 'is intending to become a major benefactor of the college.'

'Really,' said the Tutor in hushed tones. 'Who?'

'Well,' said Peter, 'knowing your policy on not discriminating against anyone, I suppose I can tell you. It's Sir Richard Mason-Legge. Awful man, but very rich. He told me he is minded to give the college a million at least if I am offered a place.'

'What!' said the Tutor. 'I don't believe it! The Master is always twittering on about that name. How do you know him?'

'I…er… am… er…quite fond of his niece. And she… is extremely fond of me…'

'I see,' said the Tutor. 'I see, I see, I see. Well, I can't promise you anything, but you are a cut above the ordinary.'

'Excellent,' said Peter. 'I knew I had made a wise decision in applying to St Badley's. I realise, of course, that much depends on the verdict of the Fellow in Economics.'

'Ah yes,' said the Tutor. 'Well, I shall look forward to my discussions with him… and the Master.'

The Porters all bade him a hearty goodbye and expressed the hope they would see him again.

'Of course you will,' said Peter. 'Go and buy yourselves a drink when you have finished your duties,' and he placed a note on the desk.

'God bless you, sir,' came the chorus. 'We shall pray for a good result!'

Back in London, Peter checked on the day's purchases of YLT. There had been a modest private order, which there hadn't been for several days, and it looked as if it had been through an Oxford broker. He called the bottom on the share price, which had moved up 1p on the strength of the strange purchase, he spread the word around the office, tipping the odd colleague elsewhere. By the end of the following morning the price was up thirty per cent. Two days later he received an offer from St Badley's.

Chapter Thirteen

A Rolls Royce drew up at the gates of St B's. An unusual sight. Inside the Porters' Lodge the Master was pacing up and down in agitation. Less of an unusual sight.

'Sir Richard! How excellent to see you! Why, you have not aged a day since... goodness is it *two* years since you last most graciously favoured us with your presence?'

Sir Richard beamed as he surveyed the Master.

'Ah, yes, *tempus fugit*. But alas, Master, though I have to say it myself, you do look a little more careworn than on our last encounter.'

'Ah, Sir Richard, if you could but know the trials and the tribulations of the academic life! Alas, we are surrounded by trivialities and obligations and paperwork and bureaucracy and tiresome undergraduates, and the chance to actually read a book is a luxury few of us can now afford. Let alone the luxury of writing one!'

'Hmmm,' said Sir Richard, pulling a pipe out of his pocket, much to the disgust of the Master. 'Shot for shit books, yes?' And he gave a knowing chuckle. The Master, puzzled, tried to pull the honoured guest out of the Lodge before he lit up. Smoking was forbidden here, and Sir Richard must surely have seen the signs. Heavens, what would the undergraduates say, when they had scored their great moral victory in getting it banned, and what would the porters say, desperate for a puff on anything, never mind a fine pipe...But if Sir Richard had seen the notices, he was intent on ignoring them completely. He struck a match, pulled leisurely on the pipe, watched the smoke curl upwards, and let out an 'aaaah, that's better!'

'Now, then,' he said, 'we have work to do, have we not, but first I wish to see an old acquaintance. Chap called Thistlethwaite. Joined you this term. Like to see what he's up to.'

'Thistlethwaite, Thistlethwaite...?' The Master was at a loss. 'Not a new Fellow, is he..? Er...the name does not ring a bell, let us ask the porters.'

Drawing himself up to his full height, and pulling on the sleeves of the gown he had put on especially for the occasion, the Master felt more secure.

'Have you got a Thistlethwaite on the books,' he demanded of the porters. 'Look him up for me, will you?'

'Mr Thistlethwaite!' The three porters were falling over themselves. 'Why of course we have, Master. Excellent man. Without doubt the best fresher in College. Splendid character! They don't come better than him!'

Sir Richard beamed. 'That sounds like Thistle,' he declared confidently. 'Where are his rooms?' The porters were now falling over themselves to accompany them to Mr Thistlethwaite's abode.

'Just a minute,' said the Master, suddenly worried that this amazing creature might live in one of the College garrets, 'perhaps I should invite him to join us in my study? Perhaps we could have a little something together?' he added, with a wink at Sir Richard.

'No, want to see him in his natural habitat,' said the latter.

'Let us take you,' urged the porters, 'he has a full set, a study and a separate bedroom, the best rooms in College!'

The Master breathed more easily. Must be a wealthy young man to afford those rooms. He had blanched at the price when his own nephew had been up. Pity the lad had failed his exams…

They were already on their way, the porters in eager competition to get there first. The Master felt uneasy, but he couldn't quite work out why. Could there be trouble ahead?

It took a minute for Peter to appear at the door. He was in his dressing gown.

'Why, M-L,' he said in delight. 'Very good to see you!' He shook the Great Man heartily by the hand. 'Come in, come in! Oh… is it the Master? Er… come in. Er, thank you, Tibbs, he said, handing over a coin from a pile by his door, oh, and you too, Bagshott.'

'No trouble whatsoever, sir,' they chorused. 'Any time at all, sir.'

'Sorry I'm not dressed for you,' said Peter. 'Bit of a late night. Essay crisis! Academic life, you know… Come into my humble abode.'

It was predictably far from being humble. Oil paintings on the walls, fine rugs, massive desk, an enormous monitor with what looked a like a graph, going sharply upwards, vases, flowers… Flowers!

'Is this college furniture?' asked the Master, a little flustered.

'Ah no,' said Peter. 'Got a few pieces of my own brought in.'

The Master's eye was suddenly caught by two fine champagne glasses and an empty bottle of Bollinger… and then, horrors, what had obviously been strewn in a hurry on one of the fine rugs: a suspender belt and a pair of stockings. He gulped in disbelief and envy. M-L saw them too.

'Damn you, Thistle,' he said. 'Up to your old tricks again! Take my hat off to you! Where is she? Through there?' And he nodded in the direction of the bedroom.

'Ah, that's for me to know and you to find out,' said Peter. 'But on second thoughts, it's just for me to know… Do sit down, M-L. Glass of the usual?'

'Splendid,' said M-L. 'What you got at the moment?'

'Will a single barrel, fifteen year-old do you?'

'Aaaaah,' said M-L, 'now you're talking. Usual quantity!'

Peter dug a bottle out of a bottom cabinet which seemed overflowing with alcohol of various varieties, and poured a small tumbler full. 'I'll get you some water for your second glass, M-L', he said, 'I've got a fridge in the bedroom.'

He went into the next room. There was some female laughter, and then he returned with a bottle of chilled Scottish Spring.

M-L had already downed his first, and was eagerly

awaiting his second. He lit up his pipe again and snorted. 'Damn good pad you got here, Thistle. Aaaah, haven't enjoyed myself as much for a week.' And he broke wind.

The Master raised his eyes to the heavens but quickly brought them back to the bottle.

'Oh, Master, would you like a drop?' asked Peter. 'Although there's a story you don't drink before sundown, is that right?'

The Master gave a wan smile.

'Oh, a wee dram won't harm me...'

'Fine,' said Peter, 'wee dram it is.' He poured a tiny amount into another glass, filled it to the brim with water, and passed it over.

The Master mumbled something under his breath.

'My pleasure,' said Peter.

At that moment they were joined by a short-skirted, long-legged, well-endowed redhead, who breezed out of the bedroom and with a 'hello, uncle', gave M-L a kiss on the forehead.

'Miranda!' said M-L. 'Well, well, well. Join us for a drink!'

'Thistle,' he commanded, 'same again all round.'

The Master quickly downed his glass, but with a worried look. Was Sir Richard better pumped for something when he was drunk or when he was sober?

The third time round the Master managed to get the glass intended for the redhead. 'Silly me!' he quipped, but by the time the clock had chimed eleven, he realised he had to make a move. He had been robbed of this damn insolent wind-breaking pipe-smoker before, only seconds before the wretch had been about to give him a million. That must not happen again. Anyway, the new Bursar would be wondering what was going on.

'Sir Richard, Sir Richard,' he bleated, 'we are having a wonderful time here, but I really wonder whether we should move on to my study, where the Bursar is waiting?'

'Ah indeed,' said Sir Richard, 'can't sit here all day chatting, time and the market wait for no man. Or *woman*,' he guffawed, 'know I've got to be politically correct here! Thistle,' he said, 'take my hat off to you. Don't know what I taught you exactly, but it can't have been bad. Only...' he said in a whisper, 'thought my niece had better taste in stockings. Blue! I ask you...'

'Sorry about that,' whispered Peter, 'but it reminds me of a particular occasion...'

'Oh, before I forget,' said M-L, 'how's F T doing?'

Peter gestured towards the large monitor. The graph clearly spoke for itself.

'As you can see, M-L,' he said with a modest air, 'it's going to be a ten-bagger at least!'

'Excellent!' cooed M-L. 'How much did I toss in? Was it half a bar?'

'It was indeed. You're my biggest shareholder, you know. If you don't come out of it with a round figure multiple, I'm a monkey's er...' he glanced at the Master, 'er... perhaps we should be moving on?'

'Why no,' said the Master, 'not at all. This financial talk is fascinating to one who slumbers patiently during the College investment committee meetings when these bores from the City come and tell us how much they have lost for us this time... Hohoho!' he quickly corrected himself, 'my idea of a joke! Our advisers are first-rate, of course, and they are most ably directed by the Bursar! But... I was just wondering, you know, first-hand information of this sort, er... should the College be investing in this little enterprise or... perhaps... even... should... er... I?'

The Men from the Real World were suddenly silent.

'Well, Master,' said Peter, 'I'm not sure whether you would er... totally approve of this little enterprise, you see, it's er...'

'Tobacco, I know!' crowed the Master. 'That's why you're embarrassed, I can tell! But don't worry! In my personal life I am quite uninhibited by these politically correct foibles of the College. People's health is their own concern!'

'No, no,' reassured Peter, 'it's nothing to do with

health, although actually, on reflection, you could say it's very much concerned with health and a sense of satisfaction and making men feel better about themselves and...'

'Men *and* women!' corrected the Master.

'Funny you should say that,' said Peter, 'because in fact we open our first centre for women overseas tomorrow. Did you know, M-L,' he continued excitedly, 'that the Singapore research suggested most of our customers would be in their late thirties! Just think of their disposable income! And then think of the margins! Miranda was out there last week. It's looking a dream!'

M-L held out his glass for a top-up.

'Damn you, Thistle,' he said, 'we must go fully global sooner rather than later!'

'My goodness, my goodness,' said the Master, 'what exciting lives you lead! Er... as I said, is there any hope for a small private investor here?'

Peter suddenly gave a wicked grin.

'Why of course, Master, of course! I can get you a very favourable rate through our brokers, I am sure. We're not quoted yet, you see, but I believe one of our investors is being forced to sell... paying a fine for insider dealing, you know, but leave it to me, I shall make sure you are treated most favourably and that you get a good number of our "B" shares for your investment!'

M-L looked on disapprovingly, almost as if he were about to take pity on the Master.

'Ah,' he commented, taking up Peter's lead, 'it would be most splendid to have such an eminent figure on our books! Indeed, Master, if it were to be known that someone of your stature were investing, why, that would propel us into a position of total respectability! But there's only one problem...'

'Oh dear,' said the Master, 'but surely it can be overcome..?'

'Well, perhaps,' said M-L, 'But I do believe there's a minimum investment level. What is it now, Thistle?'

'It's… fifty,' said Peter, brought back to earth.

'A mere fifty!' said the Master, 'why I could afford *far* more than that! Heavens, I could probably manage a thousand! Even… fifteen hundred!'

'Sorry, Master,' said Peter. 'I think we are at… er… cross purposes. It's fifty… thousand.'

The Master turned such a strange colour that M-L had to grab the bottle and pour him a generous portion.

'Ah,' said the Master, slightly regaining his colour, 'perhaps a little beyond me. You men from the City are indeed in a different league!'

'Ah yes,' said M-L, 'Thistle's a sharp card. Who'd have thought he'd got chucked out for gross moral turpitude!'

'M-L!' said Peter sternly, but with a wink that even the Master could not miss, 'that was a relative of mine!'

The Master's colour was changing again.

'What!' he shouted. 'What! I can well remember sending someone down for gross moral turpitude! Appalling! Appalling!' He stared hard at Peter. 'No one guilty of that offence can ever again become a member of this College!'

'Ah,' sighed Peter, 'as I said, a relative. But,' he went on in a pensive tone, 'one who may yet sue the College. He claimed he was stitched up by the Bursar and the Dean, I believe, and the Master, in gullible innocence or malevolent vindictiveness, whatever, chose to believe them. At least that's his story, the poor lad. I think, though, he's unlikely to sue. It would reflect so badly on the College, and so dreadfully on the Master, that even he would hesitate. But you never know…'

M-L had to pour the Master an even larger measure.

'Should we move on?' M-L suggested worriedly, more than a little concerned about the condition of the Master's heart...

The Bursar was pacing up and down in the Master's study, cursing inwardly. What on earth was that blighter up to?

Couldn't he even be trusted to bring someone from the bloody Porters' Lodge? How the hell could he possibly get a million out of anyone? The Bursar was not pleased. He knew he'd been lucky to get this job after his many catastrophes in the City, but life had turned out to be far, far worse than he'd expected. He'd had to *work*! Just then he heard guffaws and heavy footsteps. At last! He straightened his tie and put on his relaxed air for the arrivals.

'Ah, it's Sir Richard!' he said enthusiastically. 'I remember you from my days in the City. Legend in your lifetime! Absolute legend! Great pleasure to shake you by the hand again!'

'You can cut the flattery, man,' said the Legend. 'I know you're only after my money. Well, let's get on with it. I have a proposition for you.'

'That damn Bursar,' thought the Master, 'destroying my pitch!

'Ah, Sir Richard,' he said, 'you know us only too well! But you are right, we would indeed love to have a donation from you, however small, for your old college. Let us sit down and let me give you a...' he realised with discomfort that his own brand of whisky, better one though it was for the occasion, was not quite up to what they had just been drinking... 'give you an outline of what we have in mind.'

'Fire away,' said Sir Richard. 'But my scheme's better.'

'Undoubtedly, without a shadow of a moment's hesitation,' said the Master, 'but... just let me briefly outline the situation.' He was clearly befuddled by the alcohol, but he had been preparing his brief outline every night of the preceding week. He clasped the sleeves of his gown.

'Sir Richard! We had until a little while ago a very distinguished classical scholar, in fact he was Dean of the College. A man of enormous textual knowledge, unparalleled in... let me not exaggerate too much...

Oxford… the British Isles… possibly the western world. But alas, for personal reasons he left us, leaving an immense gap in our classical provision. We simply cannot replace him. The University will take years to release the funds for the post, and even then, there is the risk that the appointee might be assigned to another college. It would be a catastrophe if that were to happen. Our only hope is… to *endow* such a post, that is, to put in place the funds so that the income received would pay for that post… and ideally we would like enough money so that we could be sure we had enough to pay such a Fellow in perpetuity. *In perpetuity,*' he emphasised in hushed tones, and, just in case Sir Richard himself was a bit befuddled by the alcohol, '*for ever*! And, of course, the post-holders would be called… The Mason-Legge Scholars in Classical Antiquity! For ever! The Bursar will fill you in on the exact financial details,' he added, 'but the fund would need…' he coughed, 'a million. Nothing to you, of course, but to us, a blessing beyond compare!'

The Bursar sighed. Oh well, the Master had done his best. Not bad, though. How would the old bugger react?

'Poppycock,' said the Old Bugger. 'Load of codswollop. I know all about these so-called textual scholars. Know what we used to call them in my day? The shot for shit brigade.' He guffawed. 'Or,' he said, 'as I prefer to put it when I'm explaining it in the City, the fort for fart fuckers.' He guffawed even louder. The Master turned a funny colour yet once again. The Bursar suppressed a smile. He had told them! Why hadn't they listened to him for a change?

The Old Bugger lit his pipe. 'My idea,' he said, 'is much grander than that. Who's the most important person in an Oxbridge college?'

The Master smiled.

'Wrong,' he said. 'It's the Bursar. The Master can make a few duff decisions, appoint the wrong people, annoy the Fellows, annoy the undergraduates…' The Master's funny colour was becoming permanent. 'But it doesn't matter! Masters come and Masters go. On the other hand… if a *Bursar* makes a few duff decisions, then the college can go bust. It can go down the tubes of oblivion. *For ever*! And where has your shotting and shitting got you then?'

The Bursar smiled. 'Ah, Sir Richard,' he said, 'how right you are. I deeply appreciate your confidence, but how does your astute analysis help us…?'

'Simple,' retorted the Astute Analyst. 'I shall endow a Bursarship. In perpetuity. *For ever*! And I don't want any old failed City second-rate day trader. I want a top man. With the best salary in Oxford! I am going to give you TWO million!'

The Master and the Bursar gawped. But there was a strange look of alarm in their faces.

'Once I've done it, the idea will catch on. We'll have the Goldman Sachs Bursarship here, and the Morgan Stanley Bursarship there, but the first one will be mine and Whitehall will not be able to ignore my simple knighthood any longer!

'And the only condition is this: the Bursarship is advertised for your next academic year and I am on the interviewing panel. Oh,' he added, 'and so is young Thistle. In fact,' he mused, 'I wonder whether he should apply for the job himself… Hmm. No, he's much too bright for that.'

The Bursar sat down. So did the Master.

'Aaaah,' said Lord Mason-Legge. 'Never enjoyed myself so much in years!' He allowed the pressure of nature to have its relief, lit up his pipe, and leant back in satisfaction.

'Oh, and by the way, Master, did you say you had a whisky?'

Chapter Fourteen

Peter went back to the City as soon as he had obtained his degree. He had changed from Economics to Classics after his first year, much to the relief of certain teachers whose knowledge of the real world was a little restricted. In his final year he won a university prize for an essay on Ovid's *Ars amatoria*. He and Miranda bought a penthouse together, in a new building that overlooked his previous apartment and where the view of the Gherkin is magnificent. Frankie and Blondilocks visit the happy couple occasionally to exchange juicy gossip and financial tips, and Peter sometimes meets them separately, quite by chance, at financial conferences in places other than London. Lord Mason-Legge is getting broody as the years pass, and when he has enough whisky in him, which does not take quite so long to achieve nowadays, he begins to hint, in his not-so-subtle way, on the desirability of nephews and nieces, who might one day be able to enjoy the Mason-Legge prizes at what is now one of the richest colleges in Oxford.

Lightning Source UK Ltd.
Milton Keynes UK
UKHW010952120522
402884UK00002B/306